PENGUIN BOOKS

CHILDREN OF A BETTER GOD

Susmita Bagchi started writing in Oriya in 1982, and has published five novels, seven collections of short stories and a travelogue; she received the State Sahitya Akademi Award in 1993. Susmita lives in Bangalore with her husband Subroto; they have two daughters.

~

Bikram K. Das was formerly a professor at the English and Foreign Languages University, Hyderabad as well the National University of Singapore. His English translation of Gopinath Mohanty's Oriya novel *Paraja* was awarded the first Sahiyta Akademi Translation Prize in 1989. He lives in Bhubaneshwar.

CHILDREN OF A BETTER GOD

SUSMITA BAGCHI

Translated by Bikram K. Das

PENGUIN BOOKS

PENGUIN BOOKS

Published by the Penguin Group
Penguin Books India Pvt. Ltd, 11 Community Centre, Panchsheel Park, New Delhi 110 017, India
Penguin Group (USA) Inc., 375 Hudson Street, New York, New York 10014, USA
Penguin Group (Canada), 90 Eglinton Avenue East, Suite 700, Toronto, Ontario, M4P 2Y3, Canada (a division of Pearson Penguin Canada Inc.)
Penguin Books Ltd, 80 Strand, London WC2R 0RL, England
Penguin Ireland, 25 St Stephen's Green, Dublin 2, Ireland (a division of Penguin Books Ltd)
Penguin Group (Australia), 250 Camberwell Road, Camberwell, Victoria 3124, Australia (a division of Pearson Australia Group Pty Ltd)
Penguin Group (NZ), 67 Apollo Drive, Rosedale, North Shore 0632, New Zealand (a division of Pearson New Zealand Ltd)
Penguin Group (South Africa) (Pty) Ltd, 24 Sturdee Avenue, Rosebank, Johannesburg 2196, South Africa

Penguin Books Ltd, Registered Offices: 80 Strand, London WC2R 0RL, England

First published by Penguin Books India 2010

This is a work of fiction. Names, characters, places and incidents are either the product of the author's imagination or are used fictitiously and any resemblance to any actual person, living or dead, events or locales is entirely coincidental.

10 9 8 7 6 5 4 3 2 1

ISBN 9780143066422

Typeset in *Sabon* by Mantra Virtual Services, New Delhi
Printed at Chaman Offset Printers, New Delhi

Acknowledgements

Deba Shishu, from which *Children of a Better God* is translated, appeared in Oriya in time for the release at the silver jubilee celebrations of the Spastics Society of Karnataka. People who read the original were deeply moved by it. Then I felt that the message it carried deserved an English translation. With some trepidation, I approached Dr Bikram Das who had translated a few works of the Jnanpith Award-winning writer Gopinath Mohanty. Dr Das kindly agreed to review the original and after a few days told me that he would translate it into English.

At that stage, I reached out to Sudeshna Shome Ghosh at Penguin who agreed to a book reading in the original. Being a Bengali, it was not difficult for her to follow the narrative and sense the emotions, and she agreed to publish the translation.

I am indebted to everyone at the Spastics Society of Karnataka for taking me into their world as one of them. My deep gratitude to Dr Das for translating the original into English. Without Sudeshna and my editor at Penguin, Paromita Mohanchandra, this book would not be in your hands. Thank you so much, Sudeshna and Paromita.

acknowledgements

I must gratefully acknowledge the kindness of Shamarukh Alam Mehra, the lines from whose poem appear as those of my character, Ronnie's.

I also want to thank my husband Subroto, and my daughters Neha and Niti, for their continuous interest and involvement in the my work.

The beautiful paintings included in this book were affectionately provided by the children of the Spastics Society of Karnataka.

All proceeds from the book will go to support the cause of all these special children for whom we pray to a better God.

Susmita Bagchi
Bangalore

Painting by Namratha © Spastics Society of Karnataka

one

From where she sat on the balcony, sipping her tea, what she saw did not quite resemble Bangalore, the Silicon Alley. Anupurba gazed vacantly at what was going on across the road where another Bangalore merged itself into her world. Two elderly men, who looked like daily wage labourers, squatted comfortably on a dilapidated culvert by the roadside, beedis in hand, talking loudly. A little further on, a naked child from the slum behind, who had just received a slap from his mother, had exploded into an enormous howl. Around the corner from where he stood lay a mountain of garbage and next to it, three pariah dogs growled and snapped at each other. The discordant sound of the two men's loud conversation, the child's howling and the noise of the dogs made Anupurba restless.

What a muddle she had gotten into!

Only six months ago she had been in the US; she used to be an art teacher at the Montgomery Elementary School, she had had no time to waste; and now here she was—a prisoner to unrelenting leisure!

She remembered the day when her husband, Amrit, had returned from the office and told her in an unhappy voice, 'We'll have to go back to India, Purba.'

'To India? Really? When? For how long?' she had asked excitedly.

With a dry smile Amrit had replied, 'Looks as though it'll be for good!'

'What do you mean?'

'Well, the company is starting a Development Centre in Bangalore. I'm being asked to run it.'

'And the company expects us to simply pack up and go? It isn't that easy! You should refuse! What about the children's schooling? And my job?'

'We'll have to go, Purba. I've no choice. Our department is being wound up. I'm lucky to be getting another assignment instead of being asked to leave like so many others. Four hundred and thirty of them are losing their jobs!'

Four hundred and thirty!

Anupurba sat down, petrified.

With forced enthusiasm in his voice Amrit said, 'Are you worried, Purba? You shouldn't be! After all, you're going to be the Centre Head's wife in Bangalore. Just think of the prestige you'll have! And all the benefits! A big house to live in, a car and a driver. We'll have a good life!'

The words were not sinking in. She was lost in her own thoughts.

Did they really have to go back to India for good?

It was not as if she had no feelings for her home

country. Once in every two years, if not every other, they went on a visit with the children. But wasn't there a difference between going somewhere for a holiday and settling down there for work? They had been in the US for the last sixteen years. It was a different work culture; a different way of life and living. How would she adjust to the change? How would Amrit?

Of course, there was no question of his quitting his job. The economic situation in the US being what it was, there was little chance of finding a worthwhile new job. And their bank balance wasn't exactly overflowing that he could afford to give up his job and sit comfortably at home. Maybe her salary would suffice to pay for the grocery bills, but what about the mortgage on their home? And the loan on the SUV which they had acquired only seven months ago? No, it was simply out of the question.

~

Finally, they had to return. The house and cars were sold and their other belongings carried away by packers and shipped to India. The children, Jeet and Bobby, got their school transfer certificates and reluctantly, very unhappily, Anupurba had to give up her job.

And now time simply stretched in front of her, endlessly. The Anupurba who had never had a moment to waste was now prominently among the earth's idle and the unoccupied.

It wasn't as though she hadn't tried to find work after coming to Bangalore. But there was always that something somewhere coming in the way. It would have been best if she could have found a job in the school that Jeet and Bobby were going to, but there were no vacancies there. There was a school nearby. But it was such a chaotic, terrible place that to work there as an art teacher would have been a punishment. At last, she was offered a job by the International School. The Art Department there was worth a visit. But the school was so far away that Anupurba just couldn't think of joining. It would have taken her an hour and a half just to get there, which would mean that she could never get home before five-thirty. And what if she had to attend a teacher's meeting after work? She did not like the idea of Jeet and Bobby returning to an empty home. Finally, she had to decline.

Now it was as if Time winked at her, walking past on tip-toe. Occasionally, it stopped only to tease her and make faces.

'Amma!'

It was her maid, Kamakshi. Anupurba turned around to look at her.

'Car has come back after dropping Saab at the office. Driver is asking if you want to go out somewhere; if not, he says he'll wash the car.'

Anupurba took some time to decide. Over the years, she had got so used to a regular nine-to-five job that it was painful to stay at home all day. But where could she go every day? She couldn't possibly roam around aimlessly or simply mall-crawl day in and day out. Nor did she have such close friends in this new city that she could just drop in without a reason. Yet, she needed to do something. What that something could be was not clear to her. The one thing she knew she would need to figure out, in any case, was whether she would stay in or go out.

Suddenly, she remembered something. She got up, took a last sip of her tea and put the cup down. She went into the bedroom where she had stacked a whole bunch of half-read, old newspapers. She had read something that had fleetingly caught her attention about an upcoming event in the city. If only she could find the details—that could solve her problems for the day.

'Tell Somashekhar not to wash the car just now—I'll go out immediately,' she told her maid as she fished out the paper. 'Have you finished your work?'

'Almost. There's only the kitchen to be cleaned up.'

'Well, be quick. I'll change and leave.'

It did not take her long to change into a silk sari hand-painted with abstract black and orange flowers. She took off the hairclip and tossed it into the drawer of the dressing table and shook her head to loosen her shoulder-length hair and that revived her somewhat. She did not look her age at all. She could still pass for someone in her twenties. Anupurba applied make-up lightly and a touch of gloss on her lips, pulled her sari over her shoulder and gave her image a final look of approval before heading down. She was ready to go.

'Where to, Madam?' the driver asked. She was getting used to being 'madamed'.

'Do you know where the Fine Arts Society is, Somashekhar?'

'Yes, Madam. It's on Kumarakrupa Road, next to that big hotel.'

'That's where we'll go.'

~

It was an exhibition by the students of the local College of Art. Anupurba told herself it was bound to be interesting and somehow felt happy and excited.

It turned out to be a beautiful place, a two-storeyed stone building spread out over an entire acre. There were large exhibition halls on the ground as well as the first floor, and in addition to the office there was a library and a cafeteria. And a splendid garden all around, with a profusion of flowers in bloom.

The exhibition was as good as she had hoped it would be. There were practically no visitors. A young student trailed her to explain the exhibits for a while before giving up and letting her see things by herself. Anupurba moved from exhibit to exhibit, taking her own time to pause and reflect. After she had looked at all the paintings and the sketches closely, she bought a pencil-sketch. Coming out of the exhibition hall, she looked around. She stood on one of the stone steps, to one side, looking at the flowers. She was in no hurry to go home; it would be a while before her children returned from school.

Suddenly she felt a cold gust of wind. As she pulled at the end of her silk sari to wrap it around herself, Anupurba wondered where it came from. Everyone had told her that Bangalore had no winter. The weather did turn chilly though in the early mornings and the late nights of November and December, and sometimes even in the early part of January. But once the sun had risen and thrown off its blanket of red and orange, everything became quite cosy and pleasant. Sometimes, during this part of the year, the rains came. With that, everything changed. They brought the cold north wind. Everyone took out their quilts, blankets, shawls and sweaters overnight, as if by magic.

But today there was no rain—not even a grey cloud. Then why did she feel the chill?

Anupurba looked absently at the crowd of people going up and down the stone stairs. The cold that had made her shiver a little while ago did not seem to touch anyone else. Some did carry a light shawl, but most had no sign of anything warm on them.

A doubt crept into her mind. Had it really turned cold—or was it her own mind?

'Excuse me,' someone was trying to draw her attention. Anupurba turned around to see who it was. Dressed in a simple printed cotton sari, a woman stood looking at her curiously. Her greying hair was tied in a careless knot which hung, half undone, over her back. Hesitantly she said, 'I was wondering . . . you look familiar. Were you ever, by any chance, in Ravenshaw College, Cuttack? . . . Purba?'

'Yes . . . and you?'

'I'm . . .'

Before she could complete her sentence Anupurba shouted out excitedly, 'Shobha, isn't that you?'

'You could recognize me after all?'

'Have you kept yourself in any recognizable state?' Anupurba said. 'But how could I forget those earrings of yours with the missing pearl? You haven't replaced it?'

Goodness, how she was rambling with the excitement of meeting an old friend!

Shobha burst into a laugh. 'I'm not going to either! The earrings helped you to recognize me after all, didn't they?'

Anupurba laughed too. They used to tease Shobha endlessly over those earrings when they had been at college together. This was exactly how she had dressed even then. Her clothes were chosen with indifference. Her face was always without any trace of make-up and her hastily combed hair used to be carelessly braided. But she always wore this pair of beautiful stone-studded earrings. Whenever someone asked her about them she would say, 'My grandmother gave them to me a day before she died. I'm never going to take them off.' One day, a pearl came loose and fell off. It was never found again. Shobha neither replaced it nor did she take the earrings off. The very same earrings!

'How are you here?' Shobha asked.

'I came to see the exhibition. It was quite nice, I am glad I did. What about you?'

'I'd come to meet some people in the office here. Come, Purba, let's have coffee in the cafeteria. You're not in a hurry, are you?' Shobha pulled her by the hand.

'Not at all,' said Anupurba and the two friends walked

towards the cafeteria like they once used to years ago.

~

The cafeteria sat in the middle of a garden; it looked quite attractive with its few round glass tables and black wrought-iron chairs. There were hardly any people. A few young artists and students were absorbed in themselves and no one really noticed the two as they took an empty table away from the counter on which an ageing espresso machine sat along with a couple of jars of cookies and a juicer. Two waiters watched them settle down and it took some more time before one of them finally turned up to take the order. He was as unhurried as the atmosphere of the place. Shobha recommended the filter coffee which was supposed to be really good there and Anupurba agreed to try it.

'Tell me about yourself first, Shobha,' Anupurba said as the waiter moved away to get their coffee.

'The story of my life can be told in three sentences,' Shobha replied. 'I haven't got married. I work in a school here. I live alone. It's your turn now. You got married and went away to America. That's all I know.'

'That's where I had been all these years,' Anupurba said. 'Amrit works for a software firm and we have two boys. We came back to India just a few months ago. Amrit was transferred to Bangalore.'

'Are you working?'

'Well, I was, in America. We used to live in New Jersey, very near Princeton. I was an art teacher in an elementary school there. Now I'm doing nothing.'

'An art teacher!' Shobha's voice wavered. She was about to say something else, but instead she haltingly said, 'Isn't that wonderful! Aren't you going to work here again?'

'Not now for sure. The whole work environment was very different in America. Once you get used to that culture you can't take up just any job. I did try, it did not really work out and then I gave up the idea I guess.'

'That's true,' Shobha agreed, 'It can be very different between the US and here.'

'What do you teach in your school?' Anupurba asked.

'I don't teach, Purba. I'm the Public Relations Officer—the PRO.'

'What does a school need a PRO for?'

'Well, our school is kind of different,' Shobha said. 'Why don't you come and see it for yourself?'

'Who, me?'

'Listen, Purba,' Shobha said, with sudden enthusiasm. 'Come to our school at nine-thirty on the eighteenth. The school is having its Christmas party. Bring your husband and children along.'

'Amrit?' Anupurba said. 'Some hope! He has his office! And the children have school anyway.'

'Then you come alone,' Shobha insisted. 'You will, won't you?'

'All right,' Anupurba gave in. 'Give me the address.'

Shobha looked inside her big handbag and after fishing inside its clutter of papers, sunglasses, small change and assorted knick-knacks, she finally took out her business card from a small card-holder. It read 'Asha Jyoti'—that was the name of her school. They had finished their coffee. 'I've got to go, Purba,' Shobha said. 'There are several other places to go to before I head home.'

'Yes, let's go.'

Shobha came to her car to see Anupurba off. Before leaving she suddenly said, 'I haven't yet told you, Purba. Asha Jyoti isn't like any other school. It's a school for children with cerebral palsy. But do come, you will love the place.'

Spastic children! Anupurba felt strange—it was an uncomfortable piece of information. As she was returning home in the car, she kept thinking what an awkward situation she had walked into. She had told Shobha that she would go. Now she must.

But . . . to a school for spastics?

She had never really interacted with a spastic child. Except once in her life. It was a little girl named Kuni, daughter of a certain Mr Mohanty. They were her youngest uncle's neighbours. Kuni was born the year Anupurba had appeared for her school final examination. Anupurba was told that the doctor who delivered the baby had not used the forceps properly. Kuni had stopped breathing for a few seconds right after birth. Everyone had given up hope but, surprisingly, she had survived. However, it wasn't going to be a happy life for her or for her family. Within a few months it was apparent that Kuni had suffered permanent damage to her brain. She was a spastic child; she would have to live with cerebral palsy for the rest of her life.

That was the first time she had heard the term. Kuni would never be like other normal children. She would never be able to walk, dance or run around like them.

Mr Mohanty had once brought the child along when he came to her uncle's house for a celebration in the family. She was then about four. She had a strangely thin face. Her eyes blinked rapidly, somewhat like those of a mechanical doll. She had no control over the movements of her head. Her legs were impossibly thin. When Anupurba saw the child, a shiver had run down her body. She had never been able to forget Kuni. And now, in a few days' time, she was going to a place where every child would be someone like that little girl!

Oh God! She shut her eyes to keep out the memories.

Then suddenly, a strange thought crept into her mind. Spastic children were cripples, weren't they? Some couldn't walk while others couldn't speak. What sort of Christmas party would they have?

Oh, why had she agreed to go without thinking of all this? What was she to do now? Should she offer Shobha some excuse and just stay out of it?

She dismissed the thought at once. Since when had she become so weak? She had given her word to Shobha and would keep it, come what may. Why was she worrying so much about an event that would probably get over in a couple of hours? That thought made her feel lighter.

But on the night of the seventeenth, another problem worried her. What was she going to wear to the party? She stared at her overflowing closet. What would be right for an occasion like this? And for a place like Asha Jyoti?

After a lot of consideration she finally pulled out an old Bengal handloom sari from the bottom of her closet. Dust coloured, with a black border. Her younger brother, Nilu, had sent it to her from Calcutta many years ago. It was a gift to celebrate his first job. He had no clue about saris; he had just picked up whatever the shopkeeper had probably recommended. She had worn it a couple of times to make Nilu happy. After that it had slid to the bottom where the unused piles of clothes slowly sank like buried memories. Now this would be just right for the party next day. It wasn't expensive, nothing bright or glittery.

When Anupurba had worn it the first time, she had made it a point to wear beautiful silver jewellery to make up for its ordinariness. But none of this was required for tomorrow's event. The thin gold chain she wore every day, the small ear-tops and two pairs of very ordinary bangles would be adequate—there was no need for an ensemble.

~

Jeet and Bobby left for school in the morning. It was agreed that Amrit and she would leave together; she would drop him off at the office and then take the car to Asha Jyoti. As she had planned the day before, she wore the Bengal handloom sari she had selected with a black blouse and tied her hair with a rubber band. No make-up, not even lipstick; only a tiny bindi on her forehead. That was all.

Amrit had never seen her looking so plain and as she came out he looked at her in surprise for a moment but said nothing. So, there was she was—dressed down for a happy event in a sad place.

From Amrit's office, it wasn't a long drive. Closer to Christmas the traffic thins out in Bangalore as migrants leave for their homes in faraway states. Bangalore quietens down just enough for the locals and for people who stay back to feel the holiday season for one more time. As her car moved past the store fronts with styrofoam snowflakes and pictures of Santa Claus on his sleigh, her mind went back to the real Christmas they had begun to celebrate in their adopted land, where the white Christmas had real snowflakes and the holiday season was visible everywhere from the malls to the offices and the schools and every home.

~

Somashekhar had no trouble finding his way to Asha Jyoti. There was an inconspicuous sign at the gate, a watchman without uniform stood next to it. He simply waved at the car, asking them to go in. But Anupurba somehow felt it would be inappropriate to drive up to the school in the rather expensive-looking car. She asked Somashekhar to stop the car at the gate and got out.

From where she got down, it was probably a couple of minutes walk to the main porch. Now that she had reached the school, she felt the old awkwardness return. With as much ease as she could gather, she went down the small walkway. Up a couple of low steps and a ramp for wheelchairs by the side, the place opened up to a big hall, from the ends of which she could see doors opening to various classrooms. The floor was ordinary, the place was completely functional and in the middle of that hall, she saw the reception desk. And then she was standing in front of the receptionist.

'I want to meet Shobha Das . . .' she heard herself mutter. Just as the young receptionist was about to respond to her, Shobha herself appeared.

'Oh, you're here!' she exclaimed, half running out of the office that was right next to the reception desk. Then she stopped briefly, in surprise. How different Anupurba looked today! 'You look nice, Purba,' she said because she needed to conceal her surprise.

But Anupurba couldn't take her eyes off Shobha.

Was this the same Shobha? The other day she had been wearing a simple cotton sari—which hadn't even been starched properly—and her hair was in a sloppy bun. But look at her today! She looked tall and beautiful; the embroidered raw-silk sari flattered her. She had make-up on her face. The large, black eyes, that invited a second look, were highlighted with kohl today. There were gold bracelets on her slender wrists.

All this for the Christmas party? But wasn't this a place for people with disabilities? How could Shobha have come so elegantly dressed with kohl in her eyes, to a place of sorrow, of disability?

Anupurba said nothing. The two friends held hands for a brief moment and then she followed Shobha into the building. Her eyes took in everything. Everything was on the floor and deliberately arranged with plenty of space, around ordinary, functional flooring; the white-washed walls with a notice board, a poster announcing something or the other. It was just like any other school, better than a government-run school but not like the exclusive one Jeet and Bobby went to. Then she saw what looked like a parking lot for wheelchairs and she realized why everything—the doors, the passages—were so wide in this place.

They walked past a few classrooms and finally came into an enormous veranda. This was the venue for the party. Anupurba was struck by the contrast between the reception area, which was like a sepia photograph, and this—a riot of colours. There were balloons and streamers and other decorations everywhere. It wasn't sophisticated, but what a relief it was!

As she came closer, she registered the children. It was like a wide-angle quick view and she took it all in. The children were seated in plastic chairs of many different colours arranged in rows on all four sides of the veranda. And next to them were other children who sat in rows of wheelchairs. She looked around and felt very uncomfortable. Her apprehensions had come true. This place was just full of children like Kuni. Some were bigger. Each one had a deformity that disturbed her. Some children had heads that moved in sudden jerks down to the shoulders each time they tried to move or say something; sometimes their bodies seemed to struggle in sudden uncontrollable spasms. Some had very normal-looking faces but had deformities in their hands or legs. And there were some people who stood behind the wheelchairs, bending down to straighten the heads, cleaning an occasional drool or tightening the belts of the wheelchair. Who were they, she wondered. Parents, volunteers or professional care-givers? Then there was the excited conversation of the children. Some spoke quite normally, some had a lisp and some simply made strange noises.

After that one all-encompassing glance, Anupurba kept her eyes averted. Her insides churned. For some inexplicable reason she kept thinking of her own children, Jeet and Bobby. She wanted to see them.

'Come, sit here, Purba,' Shobha said, pointing towards a row of cushioned sofas which had been placed for the special guests.

With a forced smile on her lips, Anupurba sat down beside another guest.

'*Tum Shobha ki friend ho na?* You are Shobha's friend, aren't you?' The elderly woman sitting next to her asked her in Hindi.

'Yes, I am.'

'You were an art teacher, weren't you?' The lady blurted out and then checked herself, just the way Shobha had done on the first day, as if she was about to say something more. Then, as though she realized that her uncalled-for familiarity could have been taken amiss by the guest she added, 'I'm sorry I got carried away—I addressed you as 'tum' and not 'aap'—I hope you didn't mind. After all, I am so much older than you.'

'Oh no,' Anupurba said, 'not at all. And you are . . .'

'Shanta Mathur. I am the Principal of Asha Jyoti.'

Mrs Mathur seemed to be close to seventy and was dressed in a green Kanjeevaram silk sari with a rich gold border that draped her overweight body. The Kanjeevaram silk seemed a little out of place. But it was not just her, everyone—teachers, office staff, guests and parents—all seemed to have come to a wedding or something. That included the children. Some of the girls had flashy wide hair-bands across their heads; others wore colourful ribbons in their hair. Some of the boys wore silk kurta-pajamas even though their torsos seemed awkwardly connected to their limbs. Whatever it was, Anupurba realized she had made a mistake—this was not an occasion to dress down. But somehow, in the informality of the place, there was bonhomie and an acceptance and she started to mentally settle down and feel calmer. It did not feel as strange as the moment she had alighted from the car to walk down the pathway to the reception.

~

Soon someone made an announcement. The Chief Guest had arrived.

'Who is the Chief Guest?' she leaned over to Mrs Mathur to ask.

'Oh, our Chief Guest for today is the famous Ananda Roy.'

'Ananda Roy, the pop-singer?'

'Yes, yes, the same Ananda Roy,' there was pride in

her reply. 'He's going to sing for an hour. He has been here every year at our Christmas party for the past three years. He does not charge us a penny!'

Anupurba found it strange for a moment. What was the need to bring in a pop-singer to a place like Asha Jyoti? She was baffled. Wouldn't something sober, something probably even spiritual, be more appropriate?

~

Ananda Roy arrived in black jeans and a loud red tee-shirt. Every bit *Bangalore Times, page three.* He was accompanied by his similarly attired guitarist. The wheelchairs moved, there were *oohs* and *aaahs* and even a catcall and all kinds of gurgling sounds that were between a joyful laugh and a grunt. Some held out their twisted, deformed hands but everyone's eyes shone. Ananda Roy touched, patted and held the hands of the children as he came through the path to the centre of the big hall. A few teachers chided the children, asking them to settle down. There was a flurry of last-minute activity by the organizers to move this and bring that, before the guitarist started strumming. And then Ananda started singing. It was nothing sober and spiritual. It was a current favourite on the MTV channel, an old 'remix' of a Hindi song that made everyone go crazy.

Everyone was suddenly swaying to the music.

Then suddenly, Ananda stopped.

'I say, folks, what's wrong with you? Are we going to

have a boring Christmas party this year? Come on—let's dance! Come, Mrs Mathur, Saroja! Come on, boys and girls!'

Dance?

Was this person mad? Had he forgotten where he was, what kind of audience he was singing to? Anupurba seemed to be the only one who found it all such an out of place thing to do.

Mrs Mathur got up, a little unsteadily because of her weight, and walked slowly towards Ananda. She leaned over and said something in his ear. Did she tell him that these children cannot dance? Ananda laughed conspiratorially and then broke into another song—'*Just chill chill! Just chill!*'

And Mrs Mathur began to dance, waving her arms in awkward exuberance. Everyone else seemed to have been waiting for that cue.

Suddenly, it was like water being whipped into a wave. The children rose and a frenzy followed! There was no tune, no rhythm. Some feet fell in straight steps, others were crooked. Some hands were waved in deliberate gestures; others seemed to have a will of their own! Those who were strapped to wheelchairs were unable to dance, but they moved forward, heads shaking rhythmically, and they screamed and shrieked.

It was then that Anupurba felt someone nudging her elbow. She turned around.

It was a girl. It was impossible to tell her age from her face. She had stunted legs but the rest of her body had grown differently. Her left hand extended no more than a few inches from her shoulder and then ended abruptly. She had dark, intelligent eyes and she was telling her something. Anupurba had seen her dancing with the others, swaying with her right hand placed on her head a little while ago. She had looked like an awkward midget and Anupurba had taken her eyes away quickly, guiltily.

Why was she now tugging at Anupurba's hand?

'Aunty, come and dance with us!' Her voice was strangely sweet and clear. One just could not associate the voice with the body.

Anupurba felt a lump in her throat.

By then the other teachers had started dancing along with Mrs Mathur and the children. And even Shobha was there among them. Quite a few of the parents and guests were caught up in the wave.

'Come, Aunty!' the girl repeated.

Anupurba got up from her seat. She was not afraid to dance. Her friends always thought she danced well. But at this moment something snapped inside her. She just could not take it any more. She ran into a vacant classroom and broke down sobbing.

Painting by Manjunath and Hasneen © Spastics Society of Karnataka

two

From the time the school holidays began, Anupurba had been telling Jeet and Bobby repeatedly that they should go outside to play. 'Is the living room your playground?'

But of course they did not listen.

On the morning after Christmas, the boys started with a game of baseball inside the house. She was coming down the staircase, twisting a towel around her freshly washed hair. Seeing the two she admonished them, 'The park is right next to the house—can't you go and play there?'

But no, they wouldn't go. The other children, they claimed, took one look at their baseball bat and joked 'What's that? Bheema's war-club?' The game of cricket was more than the two boys could handle. They were bowled out as soon as they came to the crease to bat. When they tried to bowl, they confused the bowler's action with that of the pitcher in baseball. Everyone laughed at them. No, they weren't going now; they might think about it in the afternoon.

Jeet, the older boy, never said much and Bobby, playing advocate for both, said, 'We're only practising catch,

Mama, not playing ball. We'll be careful not to break anything.'

That was what he *said*. But in the very next moment, the ball slipped out of his hand and struck the cupboard behind him. The glass pane splintered and fell to the floor with a crash.

Shouting at the two boys, she was about to twist their ears when the bell rang. Kamakshi, who had been sweeping the floor, opened the front door. It was Shobha.

'Shobha, wait!' Anupurba said anxiously. 'Don't come this way, there's glass all over the floor.'

'Will you move over to the other side, madam? I'll pick up the splinters,' Kamakshi said, broom in hand.

'Be careful! Don't cut your hand now! Come, Shobha, we'll move over to the dining table.'

Avoiding their mother's frown, the boys quickly went out to the park, mumbling something under their breath. *That* was a really lucky escape!

'Sit down, Shobha. What a pleasant surprise!'

'I was visiting someone nearby—Vineet Deshmukh, our accountant. And since I had come all this way, I thought I'd look you up. Your address was in my purse.'

'Good thing you've come!' Anupurba said. 'You must stay on for lunch. We'll have a long chat afterwards.'

'I wish I could afford that luxury, Purba! I have a thousand things to do.'

'But isn't the school closed?'

'It is, but there's so much work piled up that I'll be under tremendous pressure if I don't finish it now.'

'Oh!'

'Purba, shall I tell you the truth? It's *you* I came to meet. I have come with a purpose. I need your help.'

'Help?'

'Well, not exactly help—but I've come with a request. Please don't say 'no' right away. The request isn't just from me but from Mrs Mathur as well.'

Anupurba started feeling a little uncomfortable inside. It was probably a prelude to a request for money. A donation. Anyone who heard that they had lived in America held out a hand. What did they all think? That they had returned as the Rockefellers?

'Tell me,' she said, somewhat cautiously.

'Purba, you know that some of the children in our school are good at drawing. But sometimes they feel frustrated when they try to capture forms on paper, although their ideas are brilliant.'

Oh, so it's not about a donation. Anupurba relaxed. She could vaguely guess what Shobha was about to say.

' Purba, if you could spend just a couple of hours with the children, two days a week—give them a little guidance . . . None of the staff are qualified, but they take turns with the art class. Just to keep the children engaged, not really to teach them anything. You know how things are in schools like ours. We can't afford an art teacher's salary.'

Kamakshi came with water and tea on a tray. She had cleaned up the mess the boys had created.

Anupurba drank some water and said, 'It's not the salary, Shobha.' How could she tell Shobha that she was uncomfortable and probably even afraid to spend time with spastic children? 'But taking on a regular assignment . . . What if I'm unable to come, for some reason? Or have to stop midway?'

Taking Anupurba's answer for a near-yes, Shobha said enthusiastically, 'If such a situation does arise, we'll see . . . Just give us three to four months of your time. There'll be an exhibition of the children's work in the last week of April. The Arts Council where we met the other day has agreed to provide the space. If someone is attracted by the work of our children, if we can find a sponsor, then we could think of engaging an art teacher next year. Please, won't you help?'

Anupurba could have said that she would need to speak to Amrit first. And then, without having spoken to him, she could have met Shobha a couple of days later and told her apologetically, 'Shobha, I spoke to him. Sorry, but I really cannot do it.'

But she couldn't. Despite her hesitation, she consented. When she came back to the house after seeing Shobha off at the gate she said to herself, 'It's just a matter of three or four months. It'll get over quickly.'

~

The New Year was already here. The parties had started to die down. But somehow it still felt new. Jeet and Bobby's school reopened on the fourth of January. And it was also the day for Anupurba to start at Asha Jyoti. After sending the boys to school and Amrit to office, she was getting ready to leave home when the phone rang. It was Shobha.

'Busy, Purba?'

'Not really. I was just getting ready to leave. Why?'

'I've got to go out just now, Purba. They've called a meeting at short notice. I've told Ranjana. She'll explain everything to you. And since it's your first day, she'll keep you company in the classroom.'

'No problem.' Anupurba was beginning to feeling a little nervous.

'You've met Ranjana, haven't you? Ranjana Banerjee?'

'I heard so many names at the Christmas party. Maybe we have met. I can't remember.'

'Well, that means, you *haven't* met. If you had met Ranjana once, you'd remember. She's our most popular teacher as well.'

'Really?'

'Listen, Purba. Go and see Radhika first. I'll tell her you're coming. She'll make all the arrangements.'

'But who is Radhika?'

'The girl at the reception.'

'Okay, Shobha. You don't worry. I will be all right.'

Anupurba opened her closet. Today, she could make her choice without any confusion. She had understood the dress code. She selected a mauve crêpe silk sari and walked out of the house quickly.

It was her first day—she mustn't be late. Bangalore traffic was unpredictable. But why blame the traffic—the roads were in such a mess! Flyovers coming up everywhere and there was no knowing when they would be completed. Roads being dug up endlessly on the pretext that they were being widened. The narrow temporary diversions were all choked. Traffic got jammed for the slightest of reasons. If she got held up in a jam it would take at least an hour to get out. It was best to get out of the house early. She carried a book in case she reached Asha Jyoti ahead of time.

When Anupurba reached Asha Jyoti she couldn't bring herself to take her car beyond the school gates, despite the watchman's repeated instructions. The car was parked outside, as on the first day. She just didn't think it proper to step out of her silver Honda City right in front of the reception desk.

The last time when she was here for the Christmas party, there were so many cars and two-wheelers parked inside, but today everything looked empty. At a little distance, she could only see, parked on one side, the two yellow school buses. Two cycles were parked alongside. That was it. There was no sign of any human being around.

Today, she realized that the walkway to the reception had beautiful flowering bushes on either side. Beyond them was a well-maintained garden. There in the middle of it she noticed the gardener, silently at work, unmindful that she was there. She walked up the ramp on to the veranda. Though she had seen ramps on the first day, today she noticed their profusion. Strange how every office, hotel and shopping mall in the world outside was full of staircases and no one ever thought about ramps in this country. They were such an oddity, quite unlike the many countries she had been to that were so much more handicapped-friendly.

'May I help you, ma'am?' The girl at the reception desk asked, with a smile on her lips, just as on the first day. What was the name Shobha had mentioned—oh yes, Radhika!

'Hello, Radhika! I'm Anupurba. Shobha told me . . .'

'I know, ma'am. Shobha Aunty left word.' She smiled —not your professional receptionist but she was trying. She had tied her well-oiled hair in two plaits; the flowers she wore on her hair quite matched the purple dress she wore. She looked very much a part of the whole set up and her eyes sparkled.

'Ranjana Aunty is taking a class. The next break is in another ten minutes. She'll be here then. I'd have taken you to Shanta Aunty's room, but she's out too. We've got a new Health Centre, and that's where she's gone. I'm afraid you'll have to wait a little, ma'am.' She told Anupurba all this in a single breath. It seemed she was eager to tell her all she could.

'Please don't worry about me. I've brought a book along.' Anupurba sat down and pulled the book out of her purse. She was halfway through this one by Jhumpa Lahiri and was trying to finish it so that she could start the new one by Vikram Seth.

'Will you have some tea, ma'am? Or coffee maybe?' Radhika bent forward, as though about to reveal a secret. 'Our coffee is excellent, but our canteenwalla just doesn't know how to make tea.'

Anupurba laughed. She liked the way this girl spoke. 'In that case, I'll have coffee.'

'Neela, get Madam a cup of coffee,' the girl said to

someone who looked like an attendant in a sky blue sari with a navy blue border that instantly told people about hierarchy in this country. Ayahs—that was what these people were called.

The book in Anupurba's hand was open, but her eyes were on Radhika. She couldn't have been more than twenty. Not someone you would call beautiful, but she was very pleasant.

'How long have you been at Asha Jyoti, Radhika?'

'Who, me? Ten years, ma'am,' Radhika said in a matter-of-fact voice.

Ten years! Anupurba was amazed. 'You have been wouking as a receptionist for so long . . . ?'

'Oh, you mean on this job?' She laughed. 'Not even seven months. I thought you were asking how long I've been at this school. I came here the same day Ranjana Aunty started teaching here. Shanta Aunty gave me the receptionist's job after I finished my tenth standard.' There was pride in her voice.

Anupurba looked at her with disbelief. Did that mean the girl was a spastic? Who could have guessed? Her speech was clear and from what she could see of her upper torso, she looked perfectly normal. Then she realized that the table hid her legs and Anupurba suddenly wanted to change the conversation.

'You have a beautiful name, Radhika.'

'Thank you, ma'am. Do you know, it was Ranjana Aunty who gave me this name?'

Ranjana? How come? She was about to ask, but suddenly the phone on Radhika's desk rang.

'Asha Jyoti, good afternoon! How may I help you?'

Half child, half woman. Half student, half professional.

~

'Hello!'

Anupurba looked up to see a lady smiling at her. She was probably in her thirties though it was difficult to place where. She was a beautiful woman, draped in a yellow printed silk sari. Anupurba realized she had seen her at the Christmas party. She was the woman in a designer maroon silk sari that she had admired. With the long end of the sari tied around her waist she had been dancing with the children, sometimes swirling, sometimes in step. There was a vivacity in her that was unmistakable. Then she had stopping dancing after a while to greet the guests.

'You must be Anupurba!' she said.

'Yes, and you . . .'

'I'm Ranjana.'

'Hello, Ranjana!'

'I'm sorry you had to wait, Anupurba.'

'No, no!' she protested. 'In fact, I came here early to avoid the traffic. Please do not be formal with me.'

Ranjana laughed. 'Don't worry. Just give me a moment —I'll be totally informal with you.'

Her personality charmed Anupurba. No wonder she was the children's favourite!

'Let's go then?'

Radhika was still on the telephone. Anupurba waved to her and walked out with Ranjana. But somehow, something made her turn back to look at Radhika again.

'What are you looking at, Anupurba?'

'That girl . . . Radhika . . . is she spastic?'

'Yes'.

'But her speech is so clear ! And she looks like a normal person.'

'Yes, she doesn't have a speech problem,' Ranjana said in a matter-of-fact way. 'But what you said about her looks isn't quite correct. You haven't seen what she looks like below the waist.'

'Meaning?'

'Well, Radhika has practically no legs. Many children with cerebral palsy still manage to drag themselves around, but not she. For a long time she couldn't even get into a wheelchair. Now, after a lot of therapy, she can just about wheel herself to the bathroom and even make it to the school bus.'

Suddenly Anupurba remembered something. 'Radhika was telling me you gave her the name.'

Ranjana slowed down. She looked at Anupurba's face. 'Yes, that is true. She wasn't Radhika before she came to the school.'

'What do you mean?' Anupurba was very curious.

'It's a sad story,' Ranjana replied, resuming her walk. 'Come, let's go to the Art Room. I'll tell you her story over lunch.'

The name 'Art Room' was a gross embellishment. It was a square room that somehow looked awkward. It wasn't big; maybe twenty feet by twenty feet. The walls were off-white. A few charts that had no reason to be there hung listlessly. A big window opened to an overgrown hedge outside and the first thing that Anupurba noticed was the very strangely designed grill on it. Between the window and the hedge, someone had stacked up plastic chairs that had seen better days. Inside the Art Room was a huge table with bits of coloured paper, glue and paint all over. There were probably a dozen or so chairs arranged all round it. On one side stood a smaller table with four chairs—probably for the teacher to help with small group-work. Next to it was a wooden cupboard with a door half open. Inside you could see drawing materials stacked up with reasonable care. Ranjana sat down on the teacher's chair and Anupurba took a chair across from her.

~

Ranjana explained how art worked as therapy for children with congenital disabilities and growth disorders. For them it was not just about learning how to draw and paint and enjoyment. It is actually therapeutic because these children, who have to constantly struggle with poor motor coordination, need to learn how to hold things, how to move their limbs, how to focus—unlike the normal ones who do it effortlessly. Some physically challenged children did manage to learn on their own with a little guidance, but more often it was very beneficial for them to work in pairs or as a group, to enable them to learn both motor skills and social interaction.

'Sometimes a child simply refuses to sit and work with

the others,' Ranjana said. 'They can be very moody you know. If they get upset for some reason they not only refuse to work but prevent others from working. Then we have to coax them somehow and get them to sit at a separate table.'

She took a sandwich out of her bag. 'Have half of it,' she said to Anupurba.

'No thank you, I've just eaten,' Anupurba said. 'But please go ahead.'

Biting into a corner of the sandwich, Ranjana returned to Anupurba's question about Radhika's name.

'You were talking about Radhika,' she said. 'As a matter of fact, Radhika had no name at all.'

'No name?' Anupurba was not ready for this.

Ranjana narrated the story of Radhika's life.

She was born into a really poor family. Her father was a daily wage labourer and her mother worked as a domestic help. They managed to survive, although theirs was a large family. Hoping for a boy, they had produced a succession of unwelcome girls. Radhika's mother was pregnant once again. This time, everyone had offered her hope—from the priest in the neighbourhood temple to all kinds of *pirs* and mendicants. She had tried every device to placate the divine: prayers, vows, fasts. But no son came. On the contrary, the daughter that arrived, maybe because of the mother's lack of nutrition or maybe because she was plain cursed, had no legs. Two lumps of flesh extended downwards from the thighs. They didn't know what to do. Horror gripped them. They couldn't afford any treatment—not that treatment would have made any difference. The child was brought up in utter neglect.

She had no name then. She grew up rolling in the dust like a lifeless dummy, unwanted and uncared for. When she was only two years old, someone advised her family to beg at the intersections displaying her deformed legs. As soon as the traffic lights turned red at the crossroads of Indiranagar and cars came to a halt on their way to the airport, an older sister would dash into the middle of the road. Clutching the deformed child precariously in one arm, she would extend a palm towards the car's window, making sure the occupants saw the two dusty lumps of flesh. One look at the child was enough to make stout hearts quail; some drew their heads in with a shiver, and then turned to look again at this child without legs.

Pity came easy. Business was good.

The crippled girl grew older. There was no need now for the older sister to hold her. The father had managed to find a small wooden cart with wheels. At great risk to herself, she propelled herself from one side of the road to the other, holding up her arms to beg. But when she was about eight, for some unknown reason, she refused to beg. She simply would not cooperate. That is when the torture began. They beat her, they starved her, and one day they dragged her out and abandoned her by the road side.

Ranjana had seen the child quite often as she travelled along the road; sometimes, she would reluctantly give her a coin. Then one day, when she saw the same child, wounded and sobbing in a corner, she couldn't take it any more. She stopped her auto-rickshaw, went to the child and listened to everything she had to say. Ranjana had just started working for Asha Jyoti. On an impulse, she picked up the child and carried her in the auto-rickshaw to a local orphanage. When they asked what the child's name was, Ranjana simply said, 'Radhika'.

'Then I got her admitted to our school. She's been here ever since.'

'Has Radhika always been like this?'

'Like what?'

'Cheerful, I mean.'

'Always. Sometimes I am amazed. If others had suffered the mental and physical pain she has, they would have turned bitter for life and would never have trusted another person on earth. But just look at our Radhika. Always smiling! Treating everyone as her own. Not a trace of mistrust in her. Last year she passed the class ten examination. We would have helped her to continue her studies, but Radhika isn't a very bright pupil. She couldn't have done much more academically.'

'Then?'

'The school needed a receptionist. Suddenly it occurred to us, why an outsider? We thought about it and then Mrs Mathur offered the job to Radhika. That's what you see now.'

"Where does she live? Is she still at the orphanage?'

'No, she can't live in an orphanage for children — she's past the age. Someone told us there is a home for disabled girls like her. That's where we could have tried to place her. But shortly after she started working here, her parents came to know about it and they took her home. She's the family's bread-winner now.'

'And Radhika agreed?'

'I told you—she's a very positive person. She has forgiven everyone.'

'What about you? You let her go?'

'Who was I to stop her?' Ranjana was lost in her thoughts for a moment. 'People who hadn't bothered to trace her whereabouts for ten years suddenly turned into loving, caring parents. Only out of greed, what else? I knew what the reason was, but what could I have done?'

Then as if reading Anupurba's mind, she said, 'My own life is full of uncertainties. I don't know how long I can continue working. How could I have taken Radhika's responsibility?' Towards the end of the sentence, her voice quivered.

But Ranjana regained her composure before Anupurba could ask any questions. She smiled. Then she said in a cheerful voice, 'Well, the issue is simple. Radhika needs to live somewhere. Who on earth would make a home with her? Can we find her someone who would marry her without any greed? And if that is the case, it is probably better to stay with a greedy family than a greedy stranger. In the end, it is so difficult to say what the right thing is. So we left it to her—we let her decide.'

~

The bell rang. The lunch break was over and the children would be returning soon. Ranjana collected herself. 'Anupurba, this is not one of our regular art classes,' she said. 'You will find children of all ages here. This class was formed by bringing together all the children in whom we spotted a special talent for drawing. This was done specifically with the art exhibition in mind. But that doesn't mean the others don't have talent, or that they are not good enough to participate in the exhibition. Our regular art class will also continue alongside, just as before. I will, in fact, show you the paintings done by the other children. If you feel any of them deserves to be part of this special group, we can move the child to this class.'

The children for the special art class had started arriving one by one. Some leaned on each other for support; some crawled on all fours; one child came in a wheelchair. Two others had to be carried in by the ayah. There were eleven in all. Anyway, it wouldn't be too large a class.

But Anupurba felt a churning inside her. Was she nervous? She wasn't a novice art teacher. She forced herself to look into the eyes of the children. Why wasn't she able to make eye contact? *Try again, Anupurba, try again*, she told herself. Ranjana had probably expected this and that was why she had offered to come along.

'Okay children, this is Anupurba Aunty—say good afternoon to her,' she instructed.

All of them chorused, 'G-uuu-d afternoo-oon, Aunty'.

Anupurba smiled self-consciously but felt better now.

The individual introductions took quite a while. Anupurba was slowly gaining control over herself.

Ranjana suddenly asked no one in particular, 'Where's Uma? I saw her this morning. Where did she go?'

Someone said, 'Her father came late. That's why she's late for this class.'

'Oh, all right. I want all of you to draw something and show it to Anupurba Aunty. You tell them, Anupurba—what should they draw?'

Anupurba hesitated for a moment. 'Let them . . .' she began.

Looking into her eyes, Ranjana whispered, '*Anything*. They may not be able to hold a pencil or a paint-brush but they understand everything.'

'Okay,' Anupurba said. 'Very well, children. If the impossible could be made possible, what would you like to be, or would you want to do? Can you draw that for me?'

The children's faces bent low over their sheets of drawing paper.

'Impossible made possible,' someone said.

'Yes yes,' repeated a small girl with laughing eyes—she probably came from a well-to-do family because she looked healthy—even among the children who were united in their crippling disability, one could tell which ones came from a more well-to-do home.

A grown-up boy who looked too big to be in school and had the face of an eighteen-year-old, with small eyes, rough hair and the outline of a moustache, made grunting noises when Anupurba gave out the brief—he sounded happy.

The children made constant movements—and the special thing about these children was that this always signalled engagement. They got down to work.

Ranjana busied herself in arranging the drawings that the children had done earlier inside the cupboard. Anupurba moved closer to her. 'Who's Uma?' she asked.

'One of the children selected for this class,' Ranjana replied. 'But she has a terrible temper. Her father was late in bringing her lunch today and so . . . !'

The sound of squeaking wheels made her turn around. Anupurba turned around too. Seated on a wooden plank with small wheels, propelling herself with her two hands came a thin, dark girl, some twelve or thirteen years old. Her head looked just too large for her body, but there was no other abnormality in the upper part of her body. But what Anupurba saw below her waist made her feel queasy. The girl's legs were thin and strangely twisted. Completely deformed. Poor thing!

She stopped at the door. Behind her, stood a middle-aged man, shrinking into himself.

'Why have you come here?' the girl said to him angrily. 'Now go!'

She turned around and came into the classroom. No asking for permission to enter. No sign of remorse or apology on her face because she had come late to class. She came in, unperturbed, and hoisted herself into a vacant chair with her hands. Without looking at anyone she drew out a pencil from the bag that hung around her neck.

'Hello Uma!' Ranjana said.

No answer.

'See who is here! We have a new Aunty to teach us art.'

This time Uma looked up to glance once at Anupurba,

then she asked in an irreverent tone, 'What shall I draw?'

Anupurba forced a smile on her face. Walking up to Uma, she placed a sheet of paper in front of her and patiently repeated the instruction she had given to the other children.

Uma inclined her head to listen. Then, without a word, she gripped the pencil in her left hand and started her work, as if Anupurba did not exist.

Anupurba was beginning to feel a little offended, but then she quickly checked herself. What was she doing? Taking offence at the behaviour of a child with a disability!

She walked over to the cupboard. Ranjana was still there. 'Look over these drawings later at your convenience, Anupurba,' she said. 'If you approve, we can select some of them for the exhibition.'

'Sure,' Anupurba said. Then lowering her voice, she asked, 'Uma—is her problem similar to that of Radhika?'

Ranjana's hands froze for a moment. Just as she was about to say something, came a sudden outburst of giggling from the children, followed by loud whispers.

Ranjana stood up. 'What's all this?' she said in mock anger, 'Why all this noise?'

'Ranjana Aunty, Ranjana Aunty,' a child was unable to suppress his laughter. 'Srinivas has drawn a rabbit. He says he hops like a rabbit when he walks, so one day he's going to turn into a real rabbit and hop around the whole world. Hee hee!'

Several other children laughed in unison.

The nine-year-old Srinivas said in a hurt voice, 'Bipin says he'll turn into a lion and eat me up!'

'Don't you be afraid, Srinivas,' Lata said. 'If he turns into a lion, I'll become a tiger and fight him.'

Little Bipin, who was unable to speak clearly, said something in a muffled voice which Anupurba was unable to understand. But the others were used to him; they understood him all right. There was loud laughter. Ranjana laughed too. 'Okay, that's enough,' she said. 'Time's nearly up. Finish what you've been doing!'

Through all this, Uma sat gravely, taking no part in the merriment and not saying a word to anyone, completely immersed in the paper, pencil and her crayons.

The bell rang; it was the end of school.

'Yippee!' the children shouted in joy, like children everywhere. The only difference was that instead of making a dash for freedom, these children inched their way to the school buses—limping, crawling or in wheelchairs.

Uma was the only exception. When she heard the bell she raised her head momentarily. No excitement. 'I haven't finished,' she said, addressing no one in particular, 'There's a bit left. I'll take this home and finish it there.'

'No Uma, leave it here,' Ranjana said gently. 'Anupurba Aunty will have a look at what you've done today. You can finish it when she comes back on Thursday. Is that all right?'

No answer. No sign of either acknowledgment or resentment. Uma put the sheet of drawing paper aside and began to put her things away into the bag. Then hanging the bag around her neck, she descended from the chair onto the wooden plank below in one quick practised move and pushed herself out of the classroom.

'You wanted to know what her problem is?' Ranjana was asking.

Anupurba turned her gaze away from the sight of the girl on a plank with wheels, back to her guide.

'Yes, her legs are crippled, like Radhika's—but the similarity ends there. Radhika has feelings. She communicates so well. But no one has ever seen Uma smile. No one has heard her speak pleasantly. Her parents are lower middle class people. But they have sacrificed their lives for her. With them it's always 'Uma, Uma, Uma.' She could have brought her own lunch from home like the other children, but her father works early mornings and returns in the afternoons so that she can have a hot meal. He sits beside her at lunch, watching her eat. Her mother cooks all kinds of dishes for her; on some days she comes here herself, carrying her youngest baby. But all this has no value for Uma. She behaves as though she's doing them a favour. She gets very angry with them if the smallest thing goes haywire!'

'And none of you tell her anything? She cannot be disciplined?'

'If she were a normal child we might have tried to discipline her. But what can you tell someone whose mind is imprisoned inside a crippled body? Even then, Mrs Mathur spoke to her father a couple of times and asked him not to do so much. I tried explaining things to them as well. But they're such doting parents! They think it's some sin of theirs that is responsible for Uma's suffering and so they must serve her all their lives. They send her for therapy and counselling regularly. But a fire is burning inside her.'

~

Anupurba gathered her purse, said goodbye to Ranjana and stepped out. She was no longer wondering about Uma. A sense of helplessness came upon her as she started walking towards where the car was parked. Suddenly, she felt very alone.

Somashekhar was there to pick her up. He noticed the pensive look and was curious about what Madam had been doing all day in this unusual place but he did not say anything. He was not supposed to. On the ride back home neither of them said a word.

Painting by Premchand © Spastics Society of Karnataka

three

A week and a half had passed. Now that she had three classes behind her, things were easier for Anupurba in some sense—but even then, sometimes she felt uneasy for reasons she did not quite know. She was pondering the strangeness of this feeling while getting down from her car on Thursday. In some ways, she was quite used to Asha Jyoti by now; there was no reason to be apprehensive. Anupurba told herself that she must take it easy.

The watchman opened the gates for her as usual. As she walked across the garden, she ran into Mrs Shanta Mathur, the Principal. Anupurba had not met her since that first encounter at the Christmas party.

She should have called on the Principal on her first day at Asha Jyoti, before her first class. That's how it would have been at any other school—but Asha Jyoti was unlike any other school. Here, the Principal had just so many things to attend to. She wasn't always there in her room. Somehow, Anupurba also had not really tried.

'Oh, Anupurba! I'm so sorry; I haven't been able to

meet you at all. You know, I've been frightfully busy at the Health Centre and hardly had time to breathe! I've had to go there almost every day,' Mrs Mathur said hurriedly. She came across as a very genuine person.

'Yes, I know. Ranjana told me. The Health Centre has just been started, hasn't it?' Anupurba said.

'About three months ago,' Mrs Mathur said. 'Only for the spastic children. We had started it here at first, with two full-time doctors, for our own children. But when the news spread, neighbouring children started coming. How could we refuse them?'

'Are you able to manage with just two doctors?' Anupurba asked.

'How could we? We had to appoint one more. In addition, several eminent doctors from the city volunteer their services for an hour or two every week. That's how our Health Centre is run. It's God who looks after everything; or else, who are we?' Mrs Mathur looked up at the sky and raised her hands to her forehead. 'But tell me about yourself. I hope there are no problems?'

'Oh no, not at all. In fact, I'm enjoying myself,' Anupurba said, trying to sound as enthusiastic as she could.

Mrs Mathur looked at her for a moment, as if to probe whether it was really true.

'Have you had lunch, Anupurba? You have? Well, anyway, do come to my room and have a cup of coffee while I eat before the classes begin.'

'Sure, Mrs Mathur,' Anupurba said.

The two walked over to Mrs Mathur's room.

It wasn't the kind of ornate, official-looking room that one typically expects for a school Principal. There was a large desk with a heap of papers on one side. The three visitor chairs were mismatched. A flower vase stood behind the desk up on a stool that did not fit in with the rest of the furniture. Behind the Principal's wooden chair, there was a large framed photograph of Mother Teresa, which dominated the whole room. Mrs Mathur was clearly at ease in her own place.

She took out her lunch and asked someone to send coffee. Her lunch was simple—just two dry chapattis, a bowl of moong dal, some boiled vegetables and some salad.

'I am a sackful of ailments,' Mrs Mathur said uncomplainingly. 'So I've got to live on this dry, boiled stuff. Diabetes, cholesterol, high blood pressure—they've all come and nested inside me, as if they couldn't find shelter anywhere else.' She had an amusing way with words.

'My sons wanted me to travel, to visit London and Paris, to go on conducted tours round the world. Their wives tell me that I should sit at home and watch TV, read or just relax if I didn't wish to travel. Go shopping, meet with friends. Play with the grandchildren, if there is nothing else to do. But I know very well I cannot do any of these things—not in this life. And I've been able to convince my husband. Fortunately, he's mad about golf and bridge, and so he has no complaints. He's happy with his club. I am happy too. Asha Jyoti has become my world. I can't live without it.'

Anupurba was listening intently.

'This will be my twentieth year here. And do you know, Anupurba, I had actually said 'no' before I first came here.'

Her husband had retired when she was fifty-two . Her two sons had already moved to Bangalore with their wives and children. Her two capable sons. Her daughters-in-law were more than daughters to her. Their telephone calls never stopped: 'Come over! Come and live with us! Why do you want to remain in Bombay after you've retired?' they kept saying.

After a great deal of thought, Mr and Mrs Mathur decided that indeed there was no good reason for them to stay away from the children. The house in Vile Parle was sold, they packed their belongings and came to Bangalore.

'Bombay was home after my marriage,' Mrs Mathur said. 'Thirty years I taught in the same convent school. I was the Principal of the school when we left Bombay, managing eleven hundred children. Could I have given up everything suddenly to sit quietly at home?'

Anupurba could understand the feeling. She exclaimed, 'One feels suffocated!'

'You are absolutely right!' Mrs Mathur said. 'That's exactly what happened to me. And then someone told me about this school. A trustee actually.'

She had felt uncomfortable at first, just like Anupurba had. And very nervous as well. Could she ever learn to manage a school for children with disabilities? She had no training or experience. It seemed daunting.

The trustee who had spoken to her said, 'Give it a try. If you don't like it, you can stop.'

Far from liking it, Shanta Mathur was startled when she first saw the school. Someone in the bureaucracy had taken pity and the government had given the institution an acre and a half of barren, rocky land near the edge of the city. An apology for a compound wall was put up; it was collapsing in several places. In a far corner stood the school building with a tiled roof. That was it.

Actually, it would be wrong to call it a building—it was no more than a large shed. Wooden partitions divided it into three rooms. Two of them were classrooms; the third was, in short, a multipurpose room. That was the office, the sitting room for the two teachers, the Principal's chamber—everything.

Mrs Mathur was shocked. The desk, made of crude planks, had a primitive telephone set. A cheap desk calendar sat by its side. Someone ferreted out a shaky, folding aluminium chair for her to sit on. On one side of the desk was an aged cupboard. Someone must have picked up discarded furniture. There were a few brown paper files and some pamphlets inside the cupboard, which must have been printed when the school began.

Before she sat down at her desk, Shanta took a walk around the two 'classrooms'. There seemed to be no end to surprises. There were only fifteen children in the school. Fifteen! Shanta Mathur, who had managed a school with eleven hundred students, would have to settle finally for fifteen! Crazy! It would probably be far better to stay at home and play with her grandchildren. Or follow her sons' advice to go on a world tour.

The first day had not yet ended when, at about two in the afternoon, Shanta made a phone call to the trustee. 'Excuse me, Mr Chaturvedi,' she said, 'I can't do this.'

At the other end, Mr Chaturvedi made his entreaties. 'Give it a year's time,' he begged.

'No, it's impossible,' she said. Unknown to her, Shanta's voice must have risen. 'It would be different if I was twenty-five,' she said. 'At fifty-two, I can't afford to experiment. I can't take on this responsibility. Please excuse me.'

After she had put the phone down, Shanta realized that everyone had overheard her conversation with Mr Chaturvedi. Even the children sitting on the other side of those wooden partitions. What could she do? She picked up her purse and stepped out into the veranda listlessly.

She felt something getting entangled around her right foot as she walked down the steps. Shanta was startled—it wasn't some animal, was it? Anything was possible in this wilderness. About to kick the thing away, she looked down. It wasn't an animal or anything like that. What she saw around her foot were two tiny hands.

'Don't go, Aunty! Please don't go away!' The owner of those two hands, a tiny girl of seven or eight, had dragged herself out of the classroom and crawled onto the veranda. The soft, expressive eyes were moist.

'No, I couldn't go,' Mrs Mathur told Anupurba. 'I had to stay on in that school ever since. For the sake of that small girl, Noor. Noorjehan.'

'Where is she now, Mrs Mathur?'

'Noor works in our Health Centre now,' Shanta Mathur said. For a moment she was distracted. 'So many children have moved out of our school since I took over,' she said, 'but only a few have achieved social success, as the world understands it. And of those, Noor has been our greatest success story.'

'What does Noor do?'

'Noor? She's an exceptionally bright girl. She took a course in computer applications after her BA degree in Psychology. Now she's responsible for the computerization of the records in our Health Centre. In addition, she counsels children and parents who visit the Centre. They are usually very depressed when they come to us—that's only to be expected. But Noor tells them about herself, gives them her own example. She tries to explain that although life has to be a battle for a child with cerebral palsy, all doors are not necessarily closed.' Mrs Mathur's face glowed.

'How wonderful!'

'Come with me to the Health Centre one of these days, Anupurba,' Mrs Mathur said, 'You can see the star who struck me. You should see the Centre as well.'

'I certainly will,' Anupurba said.

'Do you want to come today?'

'Today? Yes, why not? My sons will return late from school today.'

'Then I'll ask someone to take you there.'

Mrs Mathur closed her lunch box and put it aside. She drank some water out of her bottle, opened her purse and took out a couple of tablets and swallowed them.

She took her bifocal glasses out of a soft black case and started wiping them with her sari. Papers were heaped on her table. She would probably have to begin work now.

Anupurba rose to go. Classes would begin again soon after the lunch break. As she was about to leave, she paused to ask, as though remembering something, 'How long did it take you to set up this school?'

'Set up the school?' Mrs Mathur repeated, 'I think we are a work in progress. All my plans are still plans; my dreams are yet to take shape. And until that happens, how can I say the school has been set up?'

'That's true. But it must have taken you quite a while to sort things out.'

'Yes, it took seven or eight months just to get the place cleaned up. You should have seen it then—thorny bushes and stinging nettles everywhere. It wasn't safe to walk around the compound even in sandals: snakes and lizards were our constant companions. One day we even had a leopard for company.'

'A leopard?' Anupurba shivered.

'Yes. There were thick lantana bushes outside our school compound that bordered a jungle tract. The trees inside were growing wild as well. Remember, this is where Bangalore actually ended then. The leopard had probably strayed in looking for cattle. Who knows?'

'Who saw it first?'

'The two labourers we had hired to clear away the bushes inside the compound saw the leopard first. What a commotion they raised! Some of our office staff came out to see what the excitement was all about, and even some people from nearby villages came running. Someone set fire to a pile of dry leaves and someone else started banging an old steel bucket with a dry branch. Luckily for us, the leopard did no harm and scampered back into the jungle.'

'And then?'

'Then we took the government's permission to cut down some trees beyond the lantana bushes and push the jungle back a little. The wall was raised higher. The school compound was cleaned up.'

Shanta Mathur dedicated her heart and soul to the task of building up the school. More children came. The school's needs grew. The city grew too. The jungle was cut down to make way for residential colonies.

'Now this is no longer where the city ends. Bangalore has stretched out in all directions. Someone sent me a proposal—he would buy half of the land on which the school stands and the money would be used for the school building. The trustees were agreeable, but I resisted. Just as well! Could we have built this large school complex if we had sold the land? Could we have built our Health Centre?'

'But you must have needed a lot of money for the school. How did you manage?'

'My seventy-two years have taught me one thing, Anupurba. If you once make up your mind to do something, you can always find a way. Many roads will open up for you. That's what happened here as well. At first I used some of the money from my personal gratuity fund to organize a few charity programmes. When that didn't suffice, I roamed all over Bangalore with my begging bowl.'

'Begging bowl?'

'Exactly. I stretched my hand out for the school. There wasn't an office in Bangalore which I didn't visit, not a businessman I didn't call on. Someone took pity and dropped ten or twenty rupees into my bag; others fobbed me off with sweet talk. Some filled my bowl before I had even asked. We were receiving some grants from the government—but that was a mere drop in the ocean. I spoke to various NGOs, appealed to several charitable organizations. Slowly, the grants increased—that's how the school building came up. We made other arrangements. The number of students went up. More teachers were appointed. We needed more office staff—more helpers, ayahs to look after the children, gardeners. School buses to bring the children to school. Drivers had to be carefully picked for the buses. You cannot hire just anyone to drive these children. They need to be responsible and sensitive, not just while driving but in their dealings with our children. Then the Health Centre, the ambulances . . . So it has gone on, but so much remains to be done. We haven't been able to provide proper vocational courses for the children. We don't have an Art Room worth the name; we can't afford an art teacher. I would like to start a bakery unit some day so that some of these children may become employable . . .' She was talking to herself now.

Anupurba was spellbound at the thought that there

were such people, too, on this earth. Mrs Mathur could have lived in comfortable retirement, looked after by doting daughters-in-law, playing with her grandchildren. But she had chosen the path of hard work in her old age. Anupurba told herself that it was probably people like Mrs Mathur who made the world a better place. Just then she was startled by the sound of a sudden anguished scream. As both of them went out to see what had happened, her legs turned to stone. Before Anupurba could understand what was happening, Shanta Mathur went forward, pushing her aside.

A child had fallen out of a wheelchair. It was Sumana, of the second standard. Several others had reached the child ahead of Mrs Mathur. One held Sumana's head in her lap; the other was stroking her arms. The child was shaking with convulsions. Someone had inserted a rolled up piece of cloth into her mouth to prevent her teeth from biting into the tongue.

'Epileptic seizure,' Mrs Mathur explained in a muffled voice.

Anupurba trembled. Her cousin, Bunu, had been epileptic and she had often seen him, as a child, being knocked unconscious by sudden fits. The doctors had warned that he would have to be careful all his life, take medicines regularly. Bunu was twenty-eight now. He had completed his education and taken up a job, but he still had to depend on strong medicines.

This little girl was epileptic too! God!

Shanta Mathur sat gravely by Sumana's side. After the girl stopped convulsing, Mrs Mathur called out to some people in a low voice, 'Sumant, Lipika, Jagannath . . .'

They all knew what needed to be done in such a situation and were going about the routine calmly. Someone was ringing up the Health Centre, someone else was trying to inform Sumana's parents; someone had fetched water and towels. The other children who had been eating lunch nearby had moved away at someone's instruction. It was only Anupurba who did not know what to do, though she felt she had to do something. She found it embarrassing to remain a mere onlooker.

Sumana's lunch box had fallen out of her hand and Anupurba went to pick it up. The chappatis and curried potatoes which the child had brought from home lay scattered on the ground. Anupurba's hands faltered. How was she to clean all this up?

'Move aside, Madam,' the ayah who was standing nearby said to Anupurba. She held a broom in one hand and a pail in the other.

Anupurba gave her the child's lunch box and moved aside. There was nothing she could do here. She had never felt so incompetent.

Slowly, she started walking back to the art class. The visit to the Health Centre could wait.

Painting by P. Shishira © Spastics Society of Karnataka

four

It had been a busy time for Amrit and somehow—between her school, Jeet and Bobby—Anupurba and her husband had not caught up with each other for a while. Today, the two boys had gone off to see a new movie at the multiplex nearby with their friends. The boys were unable to comprehend what was so special about a multiplex that their friends were so excited about. Every small town in the US had one of those.

They would not be back until evening. Amrit and Anupurba were having tea together and she was telling him about the children at her school. *Her school?* It was a strange, fleeting question in her mind and she quickly brushed it aside.

'Are you sure you want to do this?' Amrit asked her, somewhat unsure himself.

'For now, yes. I told them that I would see it through to their art exhibition,' she replied. He did not say anything. But it was clear to him that it had been an emotional roller-coaster for her.

'Do not get too emotionally involved, though.'

'How can you say that? Whatever I do, I do it with full engagement.'

'Engagement and getting emotionally involved are two different things.'

'Yes, like you are engaged with me but not involved.'

'Purba, I am serious.'

'Yes, yes, I know.'

'It can drain you out and I do not want your stress to spill over to the boys.'

She looked at him.

'No, it won't and probably you can help.'

'How?'

'Spend a little more time with me.'

He looked at her with a surge of affection and concern. They held hands in silence and he pulled her gently closer to him.

~

As the car inched through Bangalore's snarling traffic, somehow it seemed like a longer drive than usual to the school. Somewhere along the way Anupurba must have dozed off.

'Madam,' Somashekhar said, breaking her reverie. They had reached the school.

Anupurba looked at her watch. She was a little late today. She hurried to her class.

The children were already seated. The drawing materials were there, neatly arranged on the table—

pencils, erasers, paint-boxes, brushes. Everyone was waiting for her.

'Good morning, Aunty,' they chorused in their usual mix of words, grunting noises and wheezing sounds. But they were all happy to see her and after one look at the children, Anupurba actually felt very happy to be there.

'Good morning,' she replied, 'Give me two minutes and we will all get started.'

She hurriedly took the half-finished drawings out of the cupboard and laid them on her table. The day she and Ranjana had packed them away she had not quite noticed them in any detail. As she kept the whole bunch on her table today, she realized how brilliantly colourful they were. There was something in these children; maybe it was the impairment, the frustration of being held as a permanent prisoner in an uncooperative body. When they painted, they used a profusion of colours, they used bright hues, and their flowers cheerfully dominated the entire area of whatever size paper you gave them. Their characters were always smiling and doing happy things. They were at play, they were cycling, they were dancing and in most paintings they were about the stuff normal children did every day, but would require a miracle of God for these children.

She looked at each unfinished work briefly, glanced at the child, read the name aloud, walked up to him or her and handed it back. The children could not wait to get started. This was clearly the high point of their day. To escape to another world in which their creation did not have to suffer as they did.

Soon, they were all deeply absorbed in their work. No chatter, no giggles. Only paper, pencils and colours. From time to time, there was a question for Anupurba. She went from child to child, sometimes to explain a drawing technique or show how to mix two colours to get a third. Surprisingly, she never had to repeat an instruction. The concentration and commitment of the children amazed her. They knew that even the most simple of movements —holding a pencil or keeping their bodies straight—would be a huge struggle. Yet they were completely immersed in what they were doing; the body and the mind in their harmonious best. At least for now.

Two hours just flew by. The class ended and the children left. As she put the drawings back into the cupboard, Anupurba gazed at them in wonder. What talent! She felt like going to Shanta Mathur and telling her, 'Forget about the art exhibition! I want to buy all these paintings myself.' But how could she do that? She may be able to buy up all the paintings this time, but what about the next? And the next?

No, the exhibition would have to be organized with great care. It would be something wonderful! The people of Bangalore would come to know what great talent there was at Asha Jyoti.

'Class over, Purba?' It was Shobha. She was standing at the door. Anupurba waved at her.

'Shall we go to the Health Centre? Mrs Mathur told me to take you there to meet Noor.'

'Oh yes, let's go,' she said, slinging her purse over her shoulder.

The Health Centre was at the far end, next to the school compound. From the outside, it looked tiny, but inside it was capacious. As it was for spastic children, everything was on the ground floor. There was provision for another floor but that seemed a distant possibility—only after they could afford an elevator. That too, a wide-body one, with additional safety features—so all that meant more money.

'Anupurba!' Mrs Mathur called out from her office. 'Do come in!' Ranjana was sitting next to her. They both wore reading glasses. A whole bunch of papers were piled up in front of them.

'Good afternoon, Mrs Mathur. How is Sumana?'

'She's all right. She was given an injection—something to calm the brain down. She will probably go back home today.'

'There are drugs to control epilepsy, I'm told. Is Sumana on medication of any kind?'

'She is. She's on daily medication—but the slightest thing can trigger off a seizure. All these medicines are only for seizure-control, not elimination. It's not Sumana alone—there are many others. Some more serious than the rest. Well, that's a part of our life here.'

Someone in a wheelchair, holding a file in her hand, entered the room before Mrs Mathur had finished speaking. She was dark; she wore a sky blue salwar kameez, her head veiled in a hijab. Thick glasses covered her eyes and her head was permanently bent to one side. She was probably four and a half feet in height. She spoke with a slight stammer.

'Shanta Aunty, will you have a look at this file? It's a new case. A middle-class couple has brought their daughter—in fact, it was their neighbour who forced them to come. A sad case. The couple had their first child after eleven years and the baby has cerebral palsy. The parents are in depression. I did some counselling today, but it'll take a lot of time and effort. It would be nice if you could ring them up and speak to them. They're not willing to send the girl to our school; they say she won't survive if they let her out of their sight for even a minute. The father can only work for half the day and the mother doesn't step out of the house.'

Mrs Mathur took the file out of her hand. 'I'll study the case and maybe call them up tomorrow,' she said. 'Oh yes, Noor, I want you to meet Anupurba. She has volunteered to teach our art class. Anupurba, this is our Noor. She is the star I told you about.'

'The things you say, Shanta Aunty!' Noor said, sounding very embarrassed.

'It's only the truth,' Mrs Mathur said. 'Do you think I would be here if it wasn't for you?'

'Oh!' Noor said as she was wheeling herself away. 'I nearly forgot! Ranjana Aunty, I have another counselling session the day after tomorrow, with Abdul Alam.'

'Which Abdul Alam?'

'I told you. The man from Bangladesh whose son was admitted to the fourth standard this year?'

'Oh, you mean the man who doesn't step outside the school all day?' Apparently the man would just not let the boy out of his sight. He had a premonition that something terrible would happen.

'Yes. He doesn't know a word of English and can hardly speak Hindi. I can't understand what he's saying and he can't understand me. If you're there you can speak to him in Bengali. Maybe he could open up a little if someone spoke to him in his own language.'

'The day after tomorrow? Very well, I'll come,' Ranjana said.

Noor turned her wheelchair around and left.

Mrs Mathur watched her go and turned to Anupurba with a smile. 'So now you've met our Noor,' she said. 'No more than a little girl, but she practically runs the Health Centre. If she isn't here for a day, it comes to a halt. She is both the *asha* and its *jyoti*.'

Anupurba was unable to take her eyes off the receding image of the twisted head in a hijab as the wheelchair moved away.

'Anupurba, you must be getting late. Shobha, take her round the Centre,' Mrs Mathur said. Anupurba was so lost in thought that she hardly heard what Mrs Mathur had said.

Painting by Hasneen © Spastics Society of Karnataka

five

It was well past four when Anupurba finally left the Health Centre. 'Shobha, come home with me,' she urged, tugging her friend by the arm. 'We'll chat and you can come back after dinner.'

'Not tonight, Purba. My sister is coming from Delhi on the Jet flight for an interview. She's never been to Bangalore before and her husband and mother-in-law are more worried than she is. They've been calling me repeatedly on my mobile. I must get to the airport on time.'

'Well, in that case, let's go and have a cup of coffee somewhere. Jeet and Bobby will be going for cricket coaching after school today and won't be home until half past six. I can drop you off at the airport before I go home.'

'Okay, all right.'

The two old friends had lots to catch up on. Slowly, they walked out of the gate to where the car was usually parked. There it was. Just as they were getting in, Anupurba saw Ranjana. She was desperately trying to hail an auto-rickshaw, but as usual, none were stopping at this hour.

Anupurba walked over to Ranjana.

'Ranjana, can I give you a ride home?'

'That would be wonderful,' Ranjana said. 'But you will be going to Koramangla by the Airport Road and my apartment is on Sarjapur Road. It'll be quite a detour for you . . .'

'Oh come on, it doesn't matter,' Anupurba said. 'Besides, I'm not going home now.'

'Really? It won't be inconvenient, will it? But you two friends were going somewhere together, and if you have to drop me home . . .' There was a slight hesitation in Ranjana's voice.

'No, we weren't going anywhere in particular,' Anupurba said. 'I just thought we could have coffee together somewhere and chat.'

'Come home with me then,' Ranjana said enthusiastically. 'I do not make the best coffee, but I'll make some fine tea for you.'

Shobha was perhaps about to decline but Anupurba did not notice her hesitation. 'Sure!' she said happily. 'Shobha, let's have tea at Ranjana's.'

Shobha nodded.

They had so much to talk on the way—from the proposal to relocate the airport to the nightmarish Bangalore traffic. Bangalore was no longer the Garden City it had been, although the label still clung to it. The greenery was vanishing. It would be more appropriate to call it the 'Silicon City' now. Software companies jostled each other everywhere, from the arterial roads to the narrow by-lanes with their glass and steel façades. How could the gardens have remained?

This was the easiest conversation piece and everyone among the city's inhabitants had an opinion. Ranjana said, 'It used to take me fifteen minutes to get to Asha Jyoti from my home but now it never takes less than forty-five if I start even a few minutes late. God alone knows when the Marathalli Bridge will be widened! Luckily, the traffic isn't so bad when I'm returning, or I would have gone mad by now.'

'Marathalli, what a strange name for a place!' Anupurba said.

'Well not quite,' Shobha replied. 'It is *Maratha halli* or the Maratha village. Hundreds of years back, some soldiers from Shivaji's army came and settled here. That is how the name stuck.'

'Amazing.' Trust Shobha to have such information! She always has a ready store of trivia. Then Anupurba asked Ranjana, 'How do you go home every day?'

'In my car,' she said. 'But I sent it to the workshop this morning. The brakes had been giving me trouble for some time and there was some problem with the suspension. Now I'll have to depend on auto-rickshaws for the next five days. I'll get the car back only on Friday.'

'If you can manage tomorrow and the day after, I'll be able to give you a ride on Thursday,' Anupurba said.

'Oh, don't bother,' Ranjana said.

'No bother at all. I have to get back home on Thursday,

you know. All right, you can pay me the auto-rickshaw fare if that makes you feel better,' Anupurba teased.

'Thanks!' Ranjana laughed.

Ranjana was right. Her apartment wasn't on Anupurba's route. She could have had coffee with Shobha somewhere near the airport and then driven straight home to Koramangla after dropping Shobha at the terminal. But now she would have to take the Ring Road, driving in the opposite direction to drop Shobha off.

Well, it didn't really matter. Couldn't she offer Ranjana just this little bit of help?

Somashekhar drove reasonably fast on the wide Ring Road. After he had gone a little way he turned left on the Sarjapur Road.

Anupurba stopped talking in order to survey the surroundings. This was a part of Bangalore she had not visited earlier. Many big companies had set up campuses here and apartments for their employees had sprung up on both sides of the road. The offices looked world class but the shops and apartments were a little ghetto-like. The road itself was beautifully laid out.

'Stop at the next gate,' Ranjana said. 'This is the apartment complex where I live—mine is on the fourth floor.'

'This is so nice!' Anupurba exclaimed, looking up admiringly at the ten-storeyed apartment complex. The builder certainly had some sense of aesthetics.

Shobha was silently admiring the greenery around the complex. The bougainvillea creepers were nicely raised on proud trellises. There was something elegant about the wrought-iron design that people used here, part Spanish, part Goan. Around the creepers, there was a well-kept lawn that had flower beds at the end. On the far side, there were silver oaks that separated this apartment complex from the next. There was a sense of space and openness. One did not feel boxed in as one entered.

'Come, Anupurba! Shobha, come!'

The two got down and followed her up a flight of stairs to a common arrival area and walked across to where the elevators were.

'Who else lives here with you?' Anupurba asked as they were going up in the lift.

Shobha froze and in one quick warning glance told Anupurba that she had crossed the line. Why? What was so awkward about the question?

But Ranjana was unflustered. 'No one,' she said. 'I live alone.' The elevator stopped to open its doors and the three of them quietly stepped out into the corridor leading towards Ranjana's apartment.

~

Shobha and Anupurba were quite charmed the moment they set foot inside the apartment. Ranjana had decorated it beautifully. Nothing seemed out of place; there wasn't a speck of dust anywhere. Green cushions of raw silk lay on the off-white sofa; the long curtains matched the overall colour scheme of the furniture. A large potted palm looked very healthy and happy in its corner. An original painting hung on the off-white wall, behind the three-piece sofa.

'Why don't the two of you sit,' Ranjana said. 'Let me go and get the tea.' She went into the kitchen.

Stretching out on the sofa, Anupurba asked in a low voice, 'Shobha, did I ask something I shouldn't have?'

'I'll tell you later,' Shobha whispered. 'Just remember one thing—don't ask Ranjana too many personal questions.'

'Oh.'

Anupurba picked up a book from the side table. It was a book of photographs by Raghu Rai. As she turned the pages she became thoughtful. Ranjana's apartment was certainly beautiful. Expensive too. But somehow an intimate touch was missing. There were no family photographs anywhere.

Maybe Shobha knew the answer.

She restrained herself. Why was she getting so involved in someone else's personal affairs?

'Tell me if the tea is all right,' Ranjana said. She had tea and biscuits on a tray.

'Lovely!' replied Anupurba taking a sip. 'Darjeeling?'

'Yes,' Ranjana said. 'My neighbour's brother works in a tea estate. She got me some from him.'

They chatted for some time as they drank the tea. Finally Shobha said, 'That was very refreshing, Ranjana.'

'Have another cup,' Ranjana said.

'Not today, thanks. I must get to the airport. My sister is coming to Bangalore.'

Ranjana came up to the elevator to see them off. As

the door closed, Anupurba turned round to face Shobha and said, 'Well?'

'Oh, nothing in particular,' Shobha said. 'I'd heard that Ranjana lives with a male friend. Someone at the school told me. I was feeling awkward about going to her apartment—what if he was to be at home at this time and so . . .'

She seemed to become annoyed with herself suddenly. 'My stupid middle-class mentality!' she muttered, irritated with herself.

The years she had spent in America had changed Anupurba. She wasn't particularly disturbed if someone had a live-in relationship.

'Even if it's true, how does it matter? They're not children any more, are they? But there was no sign of anyone else living there,' Anupurba said.

'Maybe Ranjana deliberately keeps her drawing room somewhat impersonal so that no one will become curious.'

'Maybe.'

'I've heard rumours that she's a divorcee. She walked out of her in-laws' home after some problems. The divorce came later.'

After a pause she went on, 'No one knows better than I how difficult it is for a woman to live alone in our society. You are right: if two adults choose to live together, it's their business. Who are we to judge?'

'Right!'

'One thing is true, though—it's difficult to find another person like Ranjana. Mrs Mathur may have laid the foundation but it is Ranjana who carries the main responsibility of managing Asha Jyoti now. It is not like she gets any special recognition for all the extra work she has to put in—she does not get paid more than the others. But she's totally indifferent to all that. She's been taking on more and more responsibility and all of it voluntarily. No—it would be very wrong to point a finger at the personal life of such a person.'

They had reached the airport.

Painting by Soumya © Spastics Society of Karnataka

six

Anupurba hardly noticed how time had suddenly grown wings all over again. Life was no longer as slow, as aimless as when she had first come to Bangalore. Even though she went only twice a week to the school—sometimes a third day—it had become the focal point of all her weekly plans. Everything seemed to somehow link itself to her going to and coming from Asha Jyoti. A week now consisted of days she went to school and days she did not, and all activities of the household arranged themselves around that.

She had not forgotten her offer to give Ranjana a ride home on the following Thursday. On the previous day, while running through the next day's plans, she reminded herself of the promise. Somehow, it was more than giving her a ride home. She actually wanted to get closer to her. So after school, as the two walked out together, they were immediately immersed in talking about a thousand things—just like long-time friends. When they reached Ranjana's home, she invited Anupurba for tea again and Anupurba readily agreed.

Ranjana unlocked the door and walked straight into the kitchen, inviting Anupurba to follow her. The kitchen was beautifully designed. Although it was not large, it looked spacious as everything was in its right place. What a difference order made! There was a small glass table in one corner, with two chairs on either side.

'Sit here, Anupurba,' Ranjana said, pulling out a chair for her. 'Let me boil the water.' The electric kettle was soon singing, she took out a china pot, measured three spoons of tea leaves and then poured the boiling water in the pot. There was a pretty tea-cosy to cover the pot—which completed the ceremony.

It was the same fragrant Darjeeling tea. Ranjana placed the cups of tea and some biscuits on the table and then sat down. After chatting for some more time about how the tea needed to steep for the exact time for the flavour to come out, Ranjana finally poured the brew into two red and blue china mugs, put a little sugar and a dash of milk in each. She stirred the liquid with slow deliberate movements of her pretty hands and offered a cup to Anupurba.

'How long have you been in this apartment, Ranjana?' Anupurba asked, sipping her tea.

'Eight years this April,' Ranjana said. 'There were no other buildings here when these apartments came up. No shops, offices or homes. The road was in bad shape. But look at the place now!'

'It still looks new after eight years!'

'The credit should go to the Residents' Association. They have been looking after things very well.'

'You must have been working at Asha Jyoti already when you moved in.' She paused. 'How did you come to Asha Jyoti, Ranjana?'

Though it was a simple question, it flustered Ranjana for a few moments. Anupurba did not know if she had crossed the line again. Slowly Ranjana gained composure. Without looking up from the cup she held clasped between both hands, she said in a soft, measured tone, 'I came to Asha Jyoti because of my daughter.'

Daughter? Anupurba's eyes involuntarily looked around quickly.

'No, there's no one here now. Soumyaa left me five years ago.' Ranjana's large, dark eyes were moist.

Anupurba was speechless. She looked at Ranjana's face. On an impulse, she touched Ranjana's hand and said, 'I'm really sorry, Ranjana. I did not mean to . . .'

'That's okay.' Ranjana's voice was surprisingly calm. 'Five years have passed. People say time heals all wounds, but this one hasn't stopped bleeding.'

Anupurba felt she ought to say something to console Ranjana, but no words came to her. She felt very guilty. Why did she have to ask this unnecessary question? Hadn't Shobha warned her?

'I keep telling myself it's a good thing Soumyaa left. She would not have survived in this harsh world. It would only have added to her suffering. It was probably a matter of time. But the way . . .'

Ranjana gazed out of the window; she was looking at the emptiness in the distance. 'Soumyaa had cerebral palsy,' she said. 'Things could have been different if she had been born into some other family,' she went on. 'She might even have survived. But unfortunately, the family felt that she was something to be ashamed of. Her affliction was a disgrace to the family. They couldn't show their faces to the outside world.'

'But this is a natural disability,' Anupurba said. 'What was shameful about it?'

A sad smile flitted across Ranjana's lips. 'You can't understand it, can you? Neither could I. How was the child to blame? Did she want to be born a spastic? Had she asked for a deformed face, for arms and legs like matchsticks? But everyone in the highly cultured, educated family was disgusted. They were united in holding her responsible for her deformity; and I, as the mother, shared the blame. My husband, Lalit, joined them.'

'Your husband?' Anupurba was stunned.

'Yes. It was one more accusation he could now pin on me. I do not know why he felt the way he did . . .' Ranjana was speaking as if in a trance.

After their marriage, Ranjana and Lalit had settled into a routine in their joint family. Small differences and disagreements did occur, but there was nothing that actually shook their relationship. The problems only arose after Soumyaa was born.

Her birth was not welcomed, there were no celebrations—the usual rituals were skipped. But when the priest performed the puja after one month, she had expected the other members of the family to be present. They all stayed away. Her mother-in-law had to go to a tambola party and her father-in-law was busy playing bridge with friends. Her eldest sister-in-law went, with her husband and children, to a birthday party at her parents' home. As for her younger brother-in-law, he was hardly ever to be seen at home. What hope could Ranjana have that he would attend? But what hurt her most was Lalit's leaving for Mumbai, on the pretext of some urgent work.

The rituals were concluded somehow. Ranjana named her baby 'Soumyaa'—the serene one. This was the name Lalit and she had agreed on before the baby's birth. If it was a son, he was to be called 'Soumya' and 'Soumyaa' if it was to be a daughter. She saw no reason to change the plans.

Her mother-in-law and elder sister-in-law smirked, 'Couldn't you think of some other name?'

Her younger brother-in-law said tauntingly, 'Call a blind boy 'Padmalochan'—the lotus-eyed one and a dark girl 'Shweta'—the fair one. And now we have a "Soumyaa"!'

Ranjana had hoped that Lalit, at least, would give her some support. But in the privacy of their bedroom he barked at her, eyes blazing, 'Were these dramatics necessary? Why did you have to call a cripple Soumyaa? What respect will I have in society? If only we could have terminated the pregnancy in time!'

She had said nothing. Turning away, she had busied herself in caring for the child. But slowly, the breach in their relationship widened, until divorce became the only way out.

She returned to her father's home. Her own kith and kin had showed some sympathy when the child was born. For a time, her anxious father had run from one doctor to another. Her mother procured ayurvedic oils for the child's massage. Her younger sister, newly married, rushed from Cochin to console her. And so, in her acute distress, Ranjana clung to her family for support. She came back home with her eighteen-month-old daughter.

Six months passed, and then a year. Gradually, sympathy changed into weariness. Ranjana noticed the same uncomfortable look in her mother's eyes that she had seen on the faces of her in-laws when friends and relations visited them. There was embarrassment.

She pretended to have seen nothing. There was no other way for her to cope.

Successions of nurses were engaged to look after the child. Some left after three months; others lasted no more than a week. The search for a care-giver would start all over again, with the lure of a higher salary. They all came and went.

The years passed slowly. Eventually, Soumyaa was eight. Ranjana heard about Asha Jyoti from a variety of sources and turned up there one day. She met Mrs Mathur. They talked. Soumyaa was admitted to the school and Ranjana was taken on as a teacher. Part-time, for the first two years, because she lacked the experience, and then one day, she was absorbed as a full-time teacher.

'Things went on, until that one day . . .' Ranjana's eyes moistened and she looked away.

That day Soumyaa was running a temperature since

the morning. Ranjana decided not to send her to school and to stay at home herself. But there was a Teachers' Meeting that afternoon. How could she not attend that? Finally, on her mother's advice, she decided to go to the school for a couple of hours, leaving Soumyaa in the care of Ratan, who had been recently engaged to look after the child.

'Those two hours became fatal,' Ranjana said.

'What happened? Did she choke or something?' Anupurba asked in a trembling voice.

When Ranjana returned home after the Teachers' Meeting, Soumyaa clung to her, sobbing. Her crying simply would not stop. Her father was getting irritated and her mother seemed indifferent. Ratan was missing; he had told them he was going out to get something from the market. Finally, Ranjana picked up the child in her arms and carried her to the clinic nearby, where Dr Nair, an elderly physician, had set up her private practice after retirement. She wasn't a specialist, but it was to her that Ranjana went whenever there was a problem. She was a good human being. The sight of Soumyaa did not make her cringe; on the contrary, she treated her with affection.

Dr Nair first gave Soumyaa some medicine to calm her down. Then she conducted a thorough examination. Something seemed to arouse her suspicion. Asking Ranjana to wait outside, she carried Soumyaa to an inner room and examined her again. Her face was grave when she emerged.

'This is shocking, Ranjana,' she said. 'But Soumyaa has been molested.'

Ranjana was horrified. Sexually molested? Who could have done this to a ten-year-old crippled child? How did it happen?

She returned home in a daze. There was no doubt who the culprit was. Ratan had not returned from the market and Ranjana knew he would never return.

'Ma, you were at home, weren't you? Then how could such a thing happen?'

The reality was that Ranjana's mother had left Soumyaa in Ratan's care and gone to her own bedroom to watch a television serial and then she had fallen asleep while it was on. Who knew that such a thing could happen in so short a time?

She flared up to hide her guilt. 'I am too old now to take on these responsibilities. Why don't you look after your child yourself? Oh my God! What a curse this child has brought to everyone!' She left the room and bolted her bedroom door. After some time, she came out and asked her accusingly, 'Now what do you plan to do?'

Ranjana picked up the phone to call the police station. It was then that both her parents objected. 'Are you in your senses, Ranju?' her father shouted. 'You want to call the police into my house because of a mentally deranged girl?'

'Soumyaa is not deranged, Baba. She understands everything.'

'Oh my God!' her father exclaimed in exasperation. 'The police today and a court case tomorrow! What respectability will we be left with? What has happened has happened. The child hasn't been harmed, has she?'

Hadn't been harmed? What greater harm could she have suffered? Ranjana looked at her father in complete disbelief.

Two days later, she walked out. Mother and daughter moved into a small rented house, not far from Asha Jyoti.

'I bought this apartment a few months later,' Ranjana said. 'I was born into one wealthy family and married into another. Whatever I may have lacked, it was not money—not so far. Life sorted itself out. But then . . .' Her eyes filled with tears again. 'Where's my Soumyaa? Her body was hollowed out by sickness, one thing followed the other, and finally she died of bronchial pneumonia . . . It's okay for her to go; children like her do not live long. But why was she violated . . . ? Maybe she would have lived longer had it not been for all that; perhaps she couldn't take the pressure any more. She was my baby . . .' Ranjana sobbed softly.

Anupurba had turned stone cold. 'I am so sorry!' was all she could say.

'I was completely broken after Soumyaa left me. No one came when she died. It was Mrs Mathur who gave me all support when there was no other help. And her nephew, Prashant.'

'Prashant?'

'He is Mrs Mathur's elder brother's son. He used to come to help out a teacher in the school. We got to know each other over time. He stood beside me at each step, gave me support. It's his help that has kept me going.'

She said nothing more and Anupurba did not want to know.

Ranjana stood up. 'I need another cup of tea. Will you have some?' she asked. Anupurba nodded.

This time, she used tea-bags. Placing a cup before Anupurba, she said suddenly, 'Prashant and I are getting married this July, Anupurba.'

'Congratulations. This is really very good news!' Anupurba needed the cheer.

'Thanks.'

'Surely Mrs Mathur knows about you two?'

'Not just Mrs Mathur, everyone in her family. Prashant's parents, his brothers and sisters—they've all known since that first day. No one has any objection.'

Why wasn't she looking happy? Why the shadow on Ranjana's face then?

She seemed to read the unasked question. 'The doubts are all in my mind. So many unknown fears! I ask myself: can I ever find happiness? Is it my fate to suffer? I never had misgivings in life but the blows life has dealt me have made me superstitious. It isn't as though I do not want to marry Prashant, but somehow, the thought makes my hands and feet go numb. I've been able to strengthen my mind after many years. You know, I have an MA in Psychology but I can't understand myself!'

Then, as though remembering something, she suddenly laughed aloud. 'Do you know who has been raising the strongest objection to my relationship with Prashant these past few years? My own parents!'

'Your parents?'

'Yes. After Prashant and I fell in love, he used to visit me every day. Two years ago, he was transferred to Pune. Even then, he comes here on work every month or so. On holidays as well. And when he comes, he stays here with me and not in his own home. I make no attempt to hide things. Everyone knows that Prashant and I live together. My parents surely know. It can't have pleased them. Family traditions, moral values, loss of character —all that stuff! If society points a finger at their daughter their own roots are threatened!'

'I've always known,' she went on thoughtfully 'that their objections would dissolve once Prashant and I decided to get married. But I was unable to accept Prashant's proposal while a doubt lingered in my mind. Who knows—maybe I had been resisting marriage so I could expose the hollowness of family traditions and disgrace my own parents socially? Then suddenly, it came to my mind: how did anybody's approval or disapproval matter to me any more? Life is too short. I must live my life on my terms. My mind was made up.'

'Will you move to Pune after your marriage?'

'Perhaps. He's trying to find a job in Bangalore. If it doesn't materialize by July, I'll resign and move to Pune with Prashant.'

Anupurba suddenly thought of Asha Jyoti. 'Asha Jyoti without Ranjana?' The words escaped her lips indistinctly. Hadn't Shobha told her that Ranjana was carrying the school on her shoulders, entirely of her own volition?

Ranjana took a deep breath. 'It will be painful to leave Asha Jyoti, I know. Let us see what plans the Lord has. But there's one thing I remind myself of always: no one is indispensable. If one Ranjana goes, many others will come.'

Painting by Deepu © Spastics Society of Karnataka

seven

Jeet and Bobby were hunched forward in front of the computer screen. These days, the two had become even closer than before. Perhaps sometimes a displacement of sorts is needed to know what people mean to each other. With the NRI tag at school and the playground, the two brothers had to create their own support system. When they were in the US, it was difficult to get the two to work together on a school project. Each had his own views on everything and before you knew it, they were fighting instead of making progress, creating problems for Anupurba. But here, they were cooperating and they did many more things together.

'Mama, my school project is on disabled people,' Jeet had informed her casually.

'That is interesting, how come?'

'I told my teacher, I would work on that one. She was asking us to think of something new and different.'

'So why disability?'

'Because Bobby and I saw so much stuff on the Internet, Mama.'

She had no idea how her work had affected the two. It was not as if she spoke a lot about her work but the household now knew a little about development disorders, cerebral palsy and, more importantly, the problem of inclusion in society that plagued everyone.

'When I grow up and become the President, there would be mandatory parking space for disabled people and ramps for wheelchairs,' the little one had declared with the assured authority of a Head of State.

'Why is India different, Mama?' the older one asked. 'Why don't people care?'

Anupurba did not have an answer. Whenever she said, 'We have many people, a big population with many problems and disability is just one of them,' the two boys did not understand. They were convinced that something was really wrong with a country in which no one seemed to care. Anupurba dreaded opinionated conclusions like that. But she also knew now that at least twelve per cent Indians had a pronounced disability and yet, no one really cared.

'Mama, that makes India the most handicapped country in this world!' Jeet exclaimed.

She said nothing. One day, she must take the boys to her school, she told herself. The only problem was that both the schools were open on pretty much the same days and had the same vacations. Should she ask them to miss class for a day, she wondered.

The phone started ringing just at that moment. It was Arunav, her brother, who had called from Cuttack. Whether they were in the US or in India, he made it a point to call every week. But his inquiries were always brief: 'How are you doing?', 'What news of the children?', 'Has Amrit returned from his tour?' The reports from his side were equally terse. It was his wife, Anupurba's sister-in-law, who would always fill in the details. And of course, her mother.

He had made his weekly phone call only two days back. This had to be out of the normal. 'Is everything all right?' Anupurba anxiously asked.

'I had told you that I would be taking Ma for a routine check-up.'

So he had. He had even joked, rather unusual for him, 'Ma doesn't agree to a comprehensive medical test. She says she's only sixty-six; she does not want us to make her feel old.'

Anupurba had tried explaining to her mother. 'Annual check-ups are common now, Ma. I had mine after I returned from the US and another one only a month ago. Does that mean I am a tottering old wreck? Ma, it's much better to be careful; who knows what could happen?'

Her mother had finally agreed after a lot of cajoling. So, what was it now that her brother was trying to convey?

'Arun, is everything normal?'

He was quiet for a moment. Then he said 'There's a blockage in her heart.'

'Blockage? What are you saying? Are you serious?' her voice was shaking.

'Purba, don't panic now. When the report showed an

abnormality I took her to Dr Mohapatra. He confirmed that there was a blockage.'

'Oh God, now what?' She was about to cry.

'Calm down and listen to me, Purba. She doesn't have any discomfort—no chest pain. But we can't afford to neglect things. Dr Mohapatra recommends an angioplasty on Monday.'

'Angioplasty? Monday? I'll get there tomorrow!' Her throat felt tight.

'Don't panic, Purba,' he tried to calm her once again. 'There's nothing to get upset about. I would have asked you to come if there was any reason to. Listen, angioplasty has become a routine procedure these days. Dr Mohapatra says she'll be back home in a day or two.'

Maybe. But her mind refused to calm down. Was he hiding something from her? Was he trying to stop her from coming because he knew Amrit was away on tour? No, she would *have* to go. If necessary, she would leave her children in a friend's care for a few days.

'No, I am coming! Ma must be in pain. You're not telling me the truth!'

'No, no, Purba. She has no pain at all. Didn't you speak to her this morning? You don't believe me? Okay then, speak to her.'

Her mother came on the line.

'What happened, Purba? Now you don't get upset. There was nothing wrong until this morning—I have no idea where all this came from!'

It was just the same, her ordinary, everyday matter-of-fact voice. No trace of pain there.

'Ma, there's no need to worry at all. Medical science has made unbelievable progress,' Anupurba said, more to convince herself.

'Who's worried? My only problem here is that Arun and Trupti will be unnecessarily bothered.'

'Shall I come, Ma?'

'No, I don't want you to be troubled. Why should you come here for just a few days? You can come with Amrit and the children during the summer holidays and stay on longer. That will be much better.'

Now she felt better after she had spoken to her mother. Her mother's voice didn't contain any panic. Whatever shortcomings they might have, in her family no one hid things from one another. Neither her mother nor her brother would lie to her.

'Ma, will you give the phone to Arun?'

'Yes, Purba?' he said.

'What time is the operation on Monday?'

'Why do you call it an operation, Purba? It isn't exactly an operation. Ma will remain conscious; only a small incision will be made under local anaesthesia and then a balloon catheter will be inserted into an artery. The catheter will open out and remove the blockage.' He was repeating to his sister what the doctors had told him.

But the sister wasn't listening.

'Okay, okay. I don't want to hear all this.'

'Don't get so upset, Purba.'

She tried to calm herself. How would her anxiety help? Removing the tremor in her voice she asked, 'When will the angioplasty thing be done?'

'At about one, may be a little after. They are still working things out. Once I know for sure from the doctors, I will let you know.'

'Arun, please call me on my cell phone the moment the angioplasty is over.'

'I will. You take care of yourself now. Bye.'

She put the phone down, but her mind remained anxious. She felt very restless inside, and she also felt very afraid. Would her mother be all right? After all, she knew so many healthy people who never recovered from even minor surgery . . .

No. No such thing could happen to her mother! Nothing would happen. Her brother had even told her this wasn't an operation. But then . . .

~

Amrit returned on Friday after spending three days in Mumbai. She usually cooked something especially for him whenever he came back from a business trip. But that day she just did not feel up to it. She did not want to do anything.

Amrit ate whatever Kamakshi had cooked. The children too were unusually cooperative that day—no fuss over 'We won't eat this—give us burgers and fries!' They knew she was very perturbed. Except for meal times, the two boys stayed in their bedroom. They took care of themselves; their homework was done before she could remind them. Even the room was spotlessly clean.

Anupurba was in no mood to talk to anyone.

Three anxious days passed. And then Monday arrived. She woke up with a throbbing headache. Was this her migraine coming back? She had suffered for eleven years, ever since she left for America, but thankfully, it had not recurred for the last five years after she had undergone homeopathic treatment.

She pressed the thumb and index finger of her right hand to her temple. A vein was throbbing away inside. How could she go to Asha Jyoti like this? If she didn't go today, would anything really happen? Should she ring up Mrs Mathur?

She got out of bed and pulled the heavy curtain aside. It looked like a nice, bright day outside.

No, she would go, she told herself.

Once she had made up her mind, it wasn't difficult. She bathed, changed into a pink Lucknow cotton sari, had her toast and orange juice as she read the newspaper and then she left. She would only fret if she remained at home—it was a much better idea to immerse herself in work.

Usually she switched off her cell phone when she entered the school but today she kept it on. Arunabh might call at any moment.

Inside the classroom, she took out the half-finished drawings and placed them in front of each child after checking the names.

Shweta had started a pencil-sketch the week before. She hadn't completed that yet. How could she? Her chattering and her giggling never stopped. Even today, she was busy tying Prabha's ribbon into a flower instead of working on her own drawing. On another day, Anupurba might have reprimanded her but today she didn't feel up to it. She simply handed out all the drawings and sat back.

She did not feel like speaking to anyone. The last time Bijon had many questions about the type of colours to use. Anupurba had told him she would show him how to mix two colours together to make a third. The moment she entered the classroom he had stammered, 'Aahnty, show me hhaaow to mmake a nnew caahllar . . .'

'Later!'

She was equally abrupt with Lata. 'Not today.'

For quite a few weeks now Lata had been dissatisfied with her own drawing. So many ideas came to her, but not a single one could she get on to paper! At times she felt like giving up the art class. She had sulked. Anupurba knew she needed to speak to her, reassure her, boost her self-confidence, but today was not the day.

Luckily, there weren't many questions from the other children today. They were all absorbed in their own work. Anupurba sat at her desk and just looked around at the classroom. All the heads were bent over sheets of drawing paper.

Except for one child. It was Uma. She was half sitting, half reclining at her desk, with her two hands resting on the desktop. Her eyes were unfocused. A corner of her drawing was fluttering in the breeze from the ceiling fan.

Anupurba's patience was running out with her. She felt annoyed. Yet she tried to calm her own voice as she asked 'What's the matter, Uma? Aren't you feeling well?'

'I'm all right,' Uma replied, gruff as usual. 'I forgot my pencil box at home.'

'Then borrow a pencil from someone.'

Uma sat with lips clenched. She wasn't going to ask anyone.

'Here, Uma! Will this one do?' Srinivas, sitting next to Uma, asked her.

She didn't even look at him.

'What's the matter? Is it too short? All right, here's another.' He took a shiny purple-coloured pencil out of his bag. 'Take this one. It's brand new.'

In a harsh voice Uma replied, 'I don't want it. You'll lend it to me now and tell me later that the point is broken or the eraser has become dirty.'

Surprised, Srinivas said 'Why would I do that?'

'Okay, okay, you needn't show how generous you are,' Uma said with a shake of her head. 'I've seen a lot of goody-goody people.'

Srinivas looked hurt. He quietly put the pencil back in his bag and went back to his drawing.

Anupurba flinched. To everyone, Srinivas was the affectionate, uncomplicated friend. Even Anupurba got a sense of it in just a matter of a few weeks. How could Uma not know that even after years of being together in the same class? Why did she have to hurt him?

Well, let her do what she pleased, Anupurba told herself. Let her sit out the entire class doing nothing. Let her go to sleep with her head on the desk. Anupurba wasn't going to tell her anything.

'Didi!'

Anupurba turned around to see who it was. A woman stood at the door. She held a two-year-old baby in her arms. Who was she? What was she doing here? Anupurba walked up to the door.

'Are you looking for someone?'

'I am Uma's mother.' She held out a pencil box, towards Anupurba. 'She left this behind at home.'

Before Anupurba could take the pencil box Uma pounced on it.

Anupurba hadn't noticed that she had clambered off her seat onto her wheeled plank and pushed herself to the door.

'Can't you arrange my things in my bag in the morning?' Uma stormed at her mother. 'Sometimes my note-book is missing and sometimes my pencil box. Are you so busy that you can't take care of my things?'

Anupurba was stunned.

'Ravi has a fever, Uma. Can't you see how he's been clinging to me since yesterday? That was why I forgot to arrange your things. Don't be angry, dear,' Uma's mother pleaded.

'You have enough time for Ravi and Sumi, but none for me!' Uma sounded very bitter.

'I made a mistake, Uma.'

'Mistake! My lunch comes late; you forget to pack my things in my school bag. Are all of you doing me a big favour or what?'

Why was she so harsh? Anupurba was shocked at Uma's attitude.

'From now on I'll have everything ready, I promise.

Please don't be angry, Uma!' Uma's mother turned to Anupurba now. 'Didi, I'll take leave now. Thank you.' She left.

Muttering to herself, Uma was wheeling herself back to her seat, making no attempt to hide her anger. She was in a rage. Her eyes were on fire.

'Uma, I want to talk to you.' Anupurba stepped in front, barring her way.

Uma stopped without a word. No remorse.

'Is that the way to talk to your mother?'

Uma looked her in the eye. There was confrontation in that look.

'That was really very rude of you,' Anupurba said.

No one had ever tried to tell Uma what to do. Not at school. Not at home. No one had ever used that tone with her. She was taken aback but did not want to show it. She was about to move on in her usual disdainful way.

'Wait!' Anupurba said again. She hadn't finished. 'The other day you misbehaved with your father, and today with your mother. You are not a small baby, Uma. You can think for yourself. Do we have to teach you how to talk to your elders? You are lucky to have such parents. You should really be grateful to God for them. But you . . . You should be ashamed of yourself. I don't ever want to see such behaviour from you. If this happens again, you will have to leave my class!'

Not a word from Uma. What did the look in her eyes suggest? Rebellion, obstinacy or plain indifference?

Anupurba made no attempt to read the expression on her face. 'Go back to your seat. Right now,' she said.

Still not a word from Uma. Slowly, she lowered her head and went back to her seat.

Anupurba was stunned at her own reaction. What had she done! Hadn't Ranjana warned her against being tough with such children? It simply wasn't the done thing. Their minds could get wounded. And here she was, not even a regular teacher in the school. And that too with a child like Uma!

Oh God!

Why did it happen? Why had she lost her calm? Was it the tension of her mother's operation?

No, she wouldn't allow herself to become agitated like this again. She turned around to look at Uma. Like the others, she was now busy drawing, she was not looking anywhere around. But why was her pencil moving so rapidly? Had Anupurba upset her?

The class ended. As usual, Uma was waiting for the other children to leave. Should Anupurba apologize to her?

Awkwardly, she went over to where Uma sat. Anupurba knew the issue remained unresolved and she needed to thaw the situation. Just then her phone rang.

She pulled the phone out of her purse frantically, saw the name of the caller and forgot everything else.

'Arun? How is Ma?'

'Everything is fine,' Arunav said. 'Let us see how long it takes before she can come home.'

'Will she go home today?'

'How can she? The doctor says Wednesday.'

'Another two days!'

'Yes. We have to do as the doctor says.'

Why did his voice sound so faint? She pressed the phone hard to her ear. She wasn't even aware of her oozing tears.

'I want to speak to her, please. Will she be able to talk now, Arun?'

'Not right now, Purba. But I'll call you as soon as she can. Don't worry.'

As she put the phone back in the purse, a surge of emotion engulfed Anupurba. She pressed both her hands over her eyes and sobbed.

After a while, she felt a presence near her and opened her eyes.

Uma!

Uma had come down from her seat quietly and moved up to her in the meantime. Anupurba composed herself. 'You haven't gone home yet, Uma? Your father must be waiting outside!'

Ignoring the question Uma asked, 'What happened, Aunty?'

Anupurba felt embarrassed. Why had she allowed her feelings to get the better of her?

She looked at Uma again. The child was waiting for an answer. Anupurba couldn't lie to her. She said briefly, 'My mother is not well.'

'Your mother? What's wrong with her?'

'There was a blockage in her heart. She had to go through something called angioplasty.'

Could the child understand all this?

'What's that? She will have an operation?'

'Actually, she has already had it. Something like an operation.'

'And if she didn't have it?'

'Her life would be in danger. She could have a heart attack any time.'

'Oh!' Uma was quiet for a moment. 'Why did this happen to her?'

'Who knows? With a problem like this, we can't always tell.'

'Oh.' She didn't say anything more but turned her wheeled plank around towards the door. She was leaning forward slightly, as though thinking of something.

Had Anupurba given her a fright by talking about her mother's illness? She closed her eyes for a brief moment. No, she needed to explain to her in more detail.

'Uma!' she called, but Uma had already gone out of the room.

~

Anupurba's mother returned home from the hospital on Wednesday. Dr Mohapatra had taken excellent care. Thank God, there were no complications. She felt relieved at last. At home, Amrit, Jeet and Bobby had been a big support. The boys made a big 'get well' card with a pink heart made of family pictures and sent it to their grandma. On Wednesday night, they all spoke to her briefly so as to give her time to recuperate.

On Thursday, when Anupurba went back to Asha Jyoti, all her anxieties were gone. She felt light and happy.

Sometimes, when you get past a difficult situation, you get new energy. Somashekhar also knew that Madam's mother was unwell and stopped near a temple on the way to school and Anupurba prayed silently for a brief moment, from outside. She promised to come again.

When she reached the school, her mind was only on the forthcoming art exhibition.

The number of children's paintings was growing by the day. A few of them would not make the mark but the rest were outstanding. She was proud of them. There was this amazing painting of blue, red and yellow concentric circles that a child had titled, 'Inside me'; in another, a sunflower field that filled up a large three-by-two sheet—it had such warmth and a certain glow! Many were abstract—but they conveyed meaning and energy—some would baffle even an art critic with their sophistication. There were a few paintings that seemed to break free and communicate with the viewer, some tugged at one's heart—like the picture of a happy foursome, two boys and two girls, with their doggie, who were sitting on a rocket and going into outer space!

When the children trooped in, Anupurba saw how eager they all were to either complete their work or to create new paintings. They were now so consumed by the entire process, that whenever Anupurba lent them a little touch here, a nudge there, it opened up their minds and all they wanted to do was keep on painting. There was magic in them.

The class ended. Anupurba was humming to herself as she got busy arranging the paintings inside the cupboard. She would show them to Mrs Mathur and Shobha. There were enough now to show how much progress had been made by her children.

'How is your mother, Aunty?'

The sudden question from a familiar voice took her by surprise. It was Uma. She had silently wheeled herself to where Anupurba stood near the cupboard. The girl's head was no higher than where Anupurba's knees were. She had concern in her eyes.

Anupurba was taken aback.

'She is much better, she will be all right,' she replied. 'She has come back home from the hospital.'

'That is so nice.'

Uma went back to her seat, as though this was all she had wanted to hear.

'Uma!' Anupurba called her from behind.

Uma turned her head around.

Anupurba walked towards Uma with long strides. She wanted to apologize.

But how? Anupurba couldn't think of the words. She only managed to lean forward and stroked Uma gently on the head. Then slowly she said, 'Thank you for asking about my mother, Uma.'

'I am happy for you, Aunty,' the girl replied.

Painting by Chhaya © Spastics Society of Karnataka

eight

Bangalore, in February, begins to warm up somewhat. People had told Anupurba that March and April were really summer months here. No doubt, the spring flowers were beginning to appear. She had never seen the purple-blue jacaranda before. Neither was the yellow tabebuia familiar to her. Then, of course, there was the very ornate red flower that sat on the lush green leaves of large trees in most neighbourhoods—no one could tell her the name. Someone had said it was flame of the forest, but she knew it was not.

Anupurba sat on her balcony sipping coffee and surveyed the landscape. Nothing had changed on the road on which her house stood. Auto-rickshaws, cars, motorcycles and scooters raised clouds of dust and deafened the ears with their noise. From the neighbouring slum came the perennial sounds of quarrelling children and the shouts of push-cart peddlers. But now her eyes saw nothing of the squalor; her ears did not register the decibel level of what would have otherwise been termed a racket. She was looking at the jacaranda tree in front of the house that was beginning to bloom with purple flowers. Some flowers had dropped from the branches, forming a carpet of purple around the foot of the tree. The colours would last for perhaps a few weeks and then vanish as magically as they first appeared. New leaves would come in their place and once again a latticed green would envelope the branches. Little birds would come and build nests. Then the wait would begin for another year for the flowers to return. Anupurba, sitting on the balcony, wanted to soak in the colours for the whole year.

Just then her mobile phone rang. She took a moment to realize it was her phone. Jeet and Bobby were perennially changing her ringtone much to her annoyance.

It was Mrs Shanta Mathur. Why this sudden call on a Friday afternoon, Anupurba wondered. She had waved to her only the day before as she was returning after her class. Mrs Mathur had said nothing then. What could have happened now?

'Hello, Anupurba. I'm disturbing you at an odd time. Please forgive me,' Shanta Mathur said.

'No problem at all, Mrs Mathur.'

'Were you resting?'

'No, I don't sleep in the afternoon.'

'I need your help, Anupurba,' Mrs Mathur said, coming directly to the point.

'Please tell me, Mrs Mathur.'

'As you know, three of our teachers have been sent to Mysore for advanced training.'

'Yes—Saroja, Prachi and Ambika. I had talked to them last week.'

'That's right. We've been planning to send them for training for the last three years, but conditions in the school have been such that I couldn't dream of sparing three of our teachers for two weeks. Fortunately, we had a large number of volunteers this year and I could afford to let them go. But a serious problem has come up this morning.'

Anupurba was listening.

'Madhumita slipped and fell in the bathroom yesterday after she returned from school and has broken her leg. She can't get out of bed now for at least a month. Harapriya had volunteered to take Prachi's classes but early this morning her mother-in-law had a severe coronary attack. She may not survive. Harapriya is in the hospital with her and I don't know when she will be able to come to the school. I was depending on Josephine, but it seems her daughter has chickenpox. She had fever for the last two days. Even then Josephine was coming to school, leaving the child in her mother's care. But now that she knows its chickenpox, she can't come. The poor girl is desperate—she knows the situation we are going through. But she might carry the infection to our children, and you know how low their immunity levels are. How can we take a risk? Can you help us out of this, Anupurba?'

'Me?' Her voice faltered.

'Yes. Can you please come every day for the next week? Saroja, Prachi and Ambika will be back next Saturday. Could you take charge of at least one class until they return?'

'Teach full-time?' Anupurba said, terrified. 'I can't, Mrs

Mathur. I know nothing about teaching these children!'

'It's not necessary to know anything,' Mrs Mathur explained. 'Bani will help you with the actual lessons. She's the class teacher for the sixth standard. As for the other things, either Ranjana or I could explain what you have to do. You won't have any problems. The important thing is to keep the children occupied until three in the afternoon.'

'And what about my art class?' Anupurba said, clutching at a straw.

'We can suspend it for this week. Please help us, Anupurba.'

Anupurba had never heard Mrs Mathur plead like this before. She could not say 'no' to her. Not at a time like this. She paused for a moment.

'I'll come, Mrs Mathur,' she said.

'Thank you, Anupurba—thank you so much!' She sounded relieved. 'Eight-thirty on Monday then. Bye now!'

As soon as she had put the phone down, Anupurba felt very anxious. True that she had agreed easily enough, but what was she to do now? How could she possibly take on such a responsibility? She had no training; she knew nothing about the curriculum for special children. How would she prepare for her classes? What was she to teach? And that too the seventh standard!

She gave Ranjana a call. Ranjana calmly explained everything to her. All classes at Asha Jyoti were extremely informal, just as her art classes had been. There were no rules, no fixed curriculum to follow, and no hard pressure of teaching. The usual school subjects were taught here

—Maths, Science, Literature, History and so on—but they were blended with lessons on everyday life which a normal, healthy child does not need to be taught.

'What do you mean?' Anupurba asked.

'Well, things like how to count money; how to shop for things; how to use a knife to cut vegetables; how to cook basic items of food.'

'The children need to learn all this?'

'Yes, they do. If they don't learn how to count money or how to shop, they can be cheated very easily. There may not always be someone to hold their hands. Not forever.'

'But cooking? Learning how to cut vegetables with a knife, lighting a stove?'

'They need to learn all that too. Most must learn to meet their basic needs without depending on anyone. If a child has the misfortune of some day living alone, she should not starve to death. There is another important thing they have to be taught here, Anupurba—how to speak to others.'

'You mean speech therapy?'

'They are given speech therapy if they need it, but at the Health Centre—not at the school. Here, they are taught the etiquette of ordinary conversation.'

'Etiquette? *These* children?'

'This is necessary in today's society. You must have noticed, Anupurba, most of our children are starved for affection. A kind word, a smile, is enough to melt their hearts. They are just as keen to show affection, but as they are unable to express their feelings clearly through words, they do so by holding the other person's hand, sometimes touching their cheeks and so on. However, there are many in our society who misinterpret these actions. There have been cases of people taking advantage of the disabilities of spastic children.'

Anupurba was horrified. It sounded repulsive.

Was Ranjana thinking too much of her own daughter? After what had happened to Soumyaa, it was natural for her to find venom concealed everywhere, in every person and in everything. Was that why such things had been made a part of the curriculum at Asha Jyoti?

Ranjana was still talking. 'You won't have to teach all this, Anupurba. Usually, I teach these topics myself, in special classes. Mukta sometimes helps me.'

'So what shall I teach? How shall I teach?' Anupurba was feeling helpless again.

'You don't have to teach anything.'

'I don't have to teach?'

'Mrs Mathur and I have discussed this. Special training is needed to teach the children at Asha Jyoti.'

'That is exactly what I tried to tell Mrs Mathur!' Anupurba interrupted Ranjana, at once feeling a great sense of relief.

But Ranjana did not seem to hear her. She went on in a matter-of-fact voice, as if she had never been interrupted. 'You can continue your art classes as before, but for these few days, you will be teaching art only in the seventh standard. You could do one thing though — teach the seventh standard children for half the day and the sixth for the other half. Bani, the sixth standard teacher, can be with her class until the lunch break and then look after the children in the seventh standard. What do you say?'

Yes, this Anupurba could do. But . . . teach the whole day? Could she manage the children?

~

In the end, her fears were unfounded.

She had barely stepped into the class when a girl rushed up to the door. Below the neck and as far as the feet, she was an ordinary twelve- or thirteen-year-old. But her head? And her face? Not a strand of hair grew on the strangely-shaped head. The scalp was totally bare. No eye-lashes. Just two small, round doll-like eyes. They did not resemble human eyes at all. Not just the eyes—the entire face looked so strange, it was like the face of someone from another planet, like an alien from a Hollywood science-fiction movie. But her face shone with excitement and eagerness. It was as though in that one moment she had found the world's greatest treasure in Anupurba.

'Hello, Aunty!' the child said, shaking both of Anupurba's hands. 'Shanta Aunty told us on Friday that we were going to have a new aunty as our art teacher. What fun! Your name is Anupurba, isn't it, Aunty? I'm sure people call you Anu. Isn't that great? People call me Anu too, but my name is Anuja.'

She said all this without a single pause—all the while shaking Anupurba's hands that were held in hers. And from then on, Anuja became Anupurba's right hand! She was her willing and extremely able assistant.

Anuja was highly intelligent. It was as if she was constantly reading Anupurba's mind. As soon as she sensed that Anupurba was in some doubt she would get up from her place, stand beside her and explain everything to her.

'Ravi can't speak, Aunty. He has some trouble with his hearing too. You will have to speak to him very loudly. Or else, you can write what you want to say to him on a slip of paper. He will write his reply on it . . . . Binita can't write. See, Aunty, the fingers of her hand are completely bent. But she can hold a pencil in her toes. She hasn't yet learnt to write with her toes, though. She's trying! That is Shahin trying to say something. She can only mumble. But I could explain to you what she's trying to tell you. I can understand all of them, Aunty. Why are you smiling, Aunty? It's true, I swear!'

She was clearly trying to imitate grown-up behaviour. Probably her mother or an aunt.

'It's true, Aunty, I can understand all of them,' she repeated.

All the children in the class laughed in unison. They were not laughing at Anuja's words but at Anupurba's attempt to suppress her amusement.

After that encounter, it was easy to relate to the children. The morning passed off smoothly enough! These children lacked the artistic talent of her art class, but they had a natural eagerness to learn. And so Anupurba did not take them into the mysteries of hues and shades but did what she could to keep them happily engaged. The short break began at half-past ten. The children at Asha Jyoti did not leave their classrooms during the short recess. They sat at their desks and munched their biscuits, an apple or whatever snacks they had brought with them. As they struggled to eat, food and saliva came out of the corners of mouth in a messy way but no one paid any attention to these things. The ayah silently wiped their faces clean and brushed away the crumbs from their clothes. The children chatted away merrily as they ate like all children everywhere, quite unmindful of the mess.

And they had so many questions to ask her as they ate. Had Anupurba Aunty really lived in America? Where? What was it like? Was it always snowing there? They had such wide streets and very big cars, didn't they? Did everyone live in big houses? Was it true that every house had a swimming pool? And yes, how was Disneyland? Were American people nice?

Anupurba tried to answer their questions patiently as she sipped the coffee which Neela had brought for her in the meantime. Sometimes she wondered about the difference between these children and the normal ones. Of late, these children no longer even 'looked' different to her!

The next class began after another twenty minutes and continued until twelve-thirty, just as in most other schools. Then the lunch break, until one o'clock.

The children scampered out of the class noisily. Anupurba was walking out behind them, but then changed her mind and went back into the classroom. She didn't feel like going to the Teachers' Common Room.

The teachers at Asha Jyoti had their own space. Anupurba had often peeped into it. But it was mostly empty, especially at lunchtime, except for a few teachers. Many who did not carry their lunch from their homes trooped into the Udupi Restaurant opposite the school. The dosa there was said to be excellent. Other teachers used the lunch break for personal errands. There were some who never left their classrooms. They had a quick bite and busied themselves in marking the children's exercise books or doing something else.

~

Anupurba had no exercise books to mark as she had been teaching art all morning. But she kept thinking of the book that Ranjana had lent her. It wasn't a storybook or a novel: it contained brief accounts of research done on spastic children.

'Mrs Mathur gave me this book to read when I had just joined Asha Jyoti,' Ranjana had told Anupurba. 'You should read it too. It will help you to get rid of several misconceptions.'

Anupurba became engrossed in it as she ate her lunch from her box. After some time, she became aware of the presence of someone at her side and raised her head. There was a woman standing close to her. She was probably in her early thirties, but had a rough face with dark circles around her eyes. The untidy knot of dry hair made her look shabby and years older. Anupurba had seen her before. She had a mythological name—was it Ahalya or Arundhati? Ranjana had told her that she was a 'special aide'.

'What's a special aide?' Anupurba had asked.

'Well, they are neither teachers nor ayahs—something in between. She's in charge of Room Number 7.'

'Is that a classroom?'

'No, it's for children who are totally crippled by cerebral palsy. These are the severe cases. They will never be able to walk or talk. But we keep trying to help them, so that they can at least sit up straight in their chairs, or scream out to their parents for help instead of soiling their own clothes. At the very least, we can help to make life a little easier for whoever is taking care of these children at home. As long as they live, they will be dependent on someone, and so Mrs Mathur has organized a special class for them. Special aides have been appointed—one for every two or three children.'

These special aides were partially educated, Ranjana had added—they had completed high school but never gone to college. The number of special aides appointed each year depended on the number of children who needed their help. All appointments were temporary. It was a tough job. The one job possibly more difficult was to be an attendant at a mental asylum.

'Would you like to see what Room Number 7 is like?' Ranjana had asked her.

'Yes, let's go.'

Room Number 7 was located at the end of the narrow passage that ran behind the school office. Different kinds of animal-like screams came from that room. Anupurba had taken a peek inside.

It was a fair-sized room. There was a big round table in one corner around which nine children sat in wheelchairs. These were not like the wheelchairs Anupurba had seen elsewhere. The wheels had been specially designed and there were restraining belts all around. The children were tied to their chairs at their waists. Their knees were tied. Their feet were tied. Still, they could not sit up straight. There was a cheap carpet on the floor on which some children lay sprawling, wearing diapers. They were perhaps seven, eight or nine years old. They rolled across the floor, trying to reach the plastic toys that lay in a corner. The children screamed, sometimes in joy and sometimes in despair. It was difficult to distinguish cries of happiness from those of pain.

Anupurba had shuddered.

'Those four women that you see—they are the special aides,' Ranjana had told her.

All four wore dark maroon salwar kameezes, which were like uniforms. Hair tightly knotted at the back of their heads, dupattas wrapped around waists so that they could rush in to help when required. There was something stoical about them as they went about delivering acts of kindness to these children who would never get any better.

That was when Anupurba had seen the woman who now stood beside her.

'Hello,' Anupurba smiled, putting the book aside.

'I am Arundhati.' There was no smile on her face. No

trace of friendliness. What was the matter?

'Sit down, Arundhati,' Anupurba said, pushing a chair towards her.

'I haven't come here to sit,' the woman said. Her eyes pierced Anupurba. She ignored the look of discomfiture that appeared on Anupurba's face. Suddenly her face grew taut. In a rough voice dripping bitterness she said, 'Why do you have to do this? You come from well-to-do families. Why do you snatch bread away from the poor?'

Anupurba was shocked. She could not speak. What kind of language was this? Why was this woman so aggressive?

She must remain calm, Anupurba told herself.

'Who are you talking about, Arundhati?' she asked. 'My name is Anupurba. I've come here just for a few days to help . . . '

'I know very well who you are!' Arundhati hissed, cutting her short. 'It's you I'm talking about. Not just you—all the others like you who have spread out their roots here. *Come here to help*, you say!' Poison dripped from each syllable, no, from each pore in her body. 'Do you know how many throats are slit because rich people like you want to help?'

Was the woman mad?

Anupurba could not swallow the insult quietly. 'What are you saying?' she said. 'What has happened?' she demanded.

'Don't you know?' Her eyes were blazing now. 'How *could* you know? Does the elephant know how many ants get crushed under its feet?'

Anupurba was annoyed now, but she calmed herself. 'You are crossing your limits, Arundhati,' she said. She did not complete what she was about to say. Someone was standing near the door.

'Hello, Anupurba! Shall we go to the sixth standard now?' Bani was at the door like a sentry guarding it.

Arundhati turned around abruptly at the sound of Bani's voice and walked out of the room with long strides.

'Why did Her Highness descend on you?' Bani asked sarcastically, watching Arundhati go. 'To shower her blessings?'

'Do you know what she was saying to me? Have you seen the way she speaks?' Anupurba was still in a state of shock.

'Of course! Who doesn't know Arundhati? She is our champion prize-fighter?'

'And still Mrs Mathur keeps her on, year after year?'

'What else can she do? She's in a tight corner. Besides, Arundhati is really good at her work, whatever her attitude may be. You should see the way she looks after those children in Room Number 7.'

'But why did she have to attack me? I hardly know her. I've never spoken to her before.'

'That's beside the point. You are a volunteer, aren't you? You are helping us without getting paid.'

Anupurba was thoroughly confused. Does one become someone's enemy because one chooses to work pro-bono, work without a salary?

'That's what *she* thinks anyway. She's convinced that

Mrs Mathur doesn't give her a permanent appointment because she can find volunteers like you, and so all volunteers are her sworn enemies. You just can't make her understand that she isn't qualified to become a teacher. Anyway, forget her. Let's go—it's nearly time.'

Anupurba's mind remained very unsettled even as she walked towards the sixth standard with Bani as her escort.

Painting by Sandeep © Spastics Society of Karnataka

nine

The unsettling saga with Arundhati did not quite end there. It was as if Arundhati had made up her mind to haunt Anupurba.

When the lunch break ended, she came and stood outside the classroom, leaning against the door. Not in the open, as one does when one wishes to talk, but stealthily, with furtive looks, inquisitive ears spread out to catch every word. She was clearly stalking her.

Anupurba felt very deeply disturbed. It was beginning to scare her. Nothing she had faced in her entire life was quite like this. At every other moment she was aware of the two blazing eyes following her, testing her, warning her. Why had Arundhati started this psychological warfare? Why was she preying on Anupurba?

Should she complain to Mrs Mathur after school hours? Let her know what was going on? But would that solve anything? What was the meaning of this stalking? Did Arundhati think Anupurba was so green that she couldn't see what was going on?

She decided to remain calm and concentrate on the

children, on the work at hand. There were only thirteen children in the sixth standard and one of them was absent today. It was no bigger than her art class. Slowly, she relaxed somewhat. She became engrossed in the paintings and in her conversation with the children.

~

The next day, she decided that she would teach the children how to make a collage out of strips of paper. But there was a problem; they were not allowed to handle scissors. How were they to cut out paper strips with scissors with their uncoordinated movements? Anupurba could do the cutting for them but what was the point unless the children themselves did it, only then would they feel that they had accomplished something. Only then could they proudly say that it was *their* collage. She was in a dilemma—whom could she ask for a solution?

One of the children guessed what was going on in her mind even before she had said a word. The badge on his shirt told her the name—Abhay. He looked the most normal of the twelve children but Anupurba learnt from the class-teacher's chart that he was the most afflicted. He had to be sent for therapy almost every day. He had already undergone two operations and would need a third after six months. Above the waist he looked healthy and his legs were like those of a normal child, but they lacked the strength to support him. Abhay couldn't move at all—he couldn't even limp or crawl, dragging his feet behind him. That wasn't all. This child, who always had a cherubic smile on his lips, couldn't speak.

It was this wordless, motionless child who found a solution to her problem. First, he tried to get her attention by tugging at the end of her sari; then, with trembling hands, he shredded a piece of paper and placed the fragments on top of each other, showing her how the task could be accomplished even without having to use a pair of scissors. Mutely he explained, this is how we do it all the time.

Anupurba understood. It was such a simple solution, yet she hadn't been able to think of it! Children with developmental disorders could make collages by using their fingers instead of sharp cutters—they converted paper into fragments and then they glued them together. She suddenly remembered Mrs Mathur telling her that shredding paper was actually a form of therapy for them.

Abhay had reminded her of what she had forgotten. But before that, he had sensed her feelings! They could anticipate so much, so well, despite being prisoners of their bodies. She felt a surge of affection rising within her. Leaning over, she ruffled the child's curly hair with her fingers.

As she was turning around from Abhay's wheelchair towards Sivaraman, she saw someone standing near the door, as motionless as a stone statue. Arundhati! She was back again, and was staring at her.

The sense of contentment she had experienced a moment ago vanished. She was being followed and watched. She could feel her body become tense. She was angry and wanted to give Arundhati a piece of her mind, but before she could speak a word the figure had turned around and left.

'Hey, you,' she wanted to shout after her. But the words remained stuck in her throat. Had she really seen something or only imagined it? Was it a trick played by the afternoon sun streaming in through the window? Was this place making her paranoid?

However, she was sure it was Arundhati and for a moment she had a very strange feeling that she had seen tears in her eyes.

~

'Purba,' Amrit called softly as he switched off the reading light. He always read a book before going to sleep.

'Ummm,' Anupurba was only half asleep.

'Are you asleep yet?'

'No, not yet.'

'Tell me about your school. What is going on?'

'Why do you want to know? You have no time for me these days.' She actually did not have a good reason to say that.

'But you are so busy and the days you go there, you come back tired. This school thing is overwhelming you way too much.'

Amrit was right. It was beginning to engulf her a lot more than she had thought.

She turned towards his side of the bed and took his hand in hers. They had always been a great support to each other. She needed him a lot more now because of what she was going through.

She told Amrit about Arundhati and what was happening in school.

'Why have you not alerted the school Principal yet? What if this loony woman ends up doing some crazy thing?' He was extremely concerned about her safety now.

'Maybe I should.'

'Do you want me to come along?'

'No,' she replied laughingly—the way she spoke when amused or embarrassed.

'I am serious.'

'Come on, I can handle it. I can handle tougher things'

'Like?'

'Like you,' she pressed her thumb on his chest.

They both laughed, knowing everything would be all right.

~

She had forgotten all about the events of the previous day when she came to school on Wednesday. She spent the first half of the morning with the students of the seventh standard like the two previous days. After the lunch break she went to the sixth. That class had only just begun when she heard a loud groan from Abhay. He had stopped shredding his sheet of red handmade paper and seemed to be in pain. Before Anupurba could understand what was happening, he had slipped out of his wheelchair, his face convulsed and his eyes glazed. Blood from his split lower lip splattered his white shirt.

Anupurba experienced a sudden jolt but did not lose her nerve. It was an epileptic seizure. Just like what she had seen Sumana go through the day she was going to visit the Health Centre. She took Abhay's head in her lap, grabbed her own clean handkerchief and put it in a bundle between his teeth. The boy was not responding; he was unconscious. He had the jerky convulsion again and some saliva spattered over Anupurba. She could smell his body odour now and surprisingly, it did not matter to her. She shouted out to Venkatesh, who was taking a class in the adjoining room, for help. He came running. In a flash, many more arrived. It was amazing how the emergency response system worked in this place. It was like an interconnected intelligence that sent out an invisible alert and help came rushing from all directions. Even Mrs Mathur appeared in a matter of minutes. Abhay was carried to the Health Centre in a stretcher. The crowd dispersed. As she was leaving, Mrs Mathur patted her on the back.

'Very well done, Anupurba! I could not have done better.'

'Thanks,' Anupurba said feebly.

The other children were completely silent.

She went out to the water tap and cleaned her sari. She washed Abhay's saliva and blood from her hands. Strange, but she was not repulsed at all. After breathing in the fresh air outside, she realized she was not in a state of high alert any more. Her breathing had returned to normal. Walking slowly she returned to the class.

'Okay, back to work!' Anupurba told the children. 'Put the collage aside. We'll do something else today. Have you children heard of origami?' She tried her best to sound natural.

No, no one had told them about origami. The children stared at her in silence.

Anupurba wrote the word on the blackboard so they could slowly re-engage their minds. As she turned back, she saw someone near the door. It was Arundhati.

She had probably been standing there for quite some time. Had she come when Abhay had his seizure? Perhaps she was watching to see how Anupurba handled the situation.

Anupurba should have been annoyed but Abhay's seizure had left her drained. There was no energy left in her for anger. She looked straight at Arundhati, prepared to meet her venomous looks and taunting words.

But there was nothing. There was no animosity in the eyes that on previous days had shone with confused anger and hatred.

Anupurba turned towards the children. After the tumultuous day, nothing could affect her. Arundhati's presence did not matter any longer.

~

After school, Anupurba walked towards the gate. First though, she had to visit the Health Centre and see how

Abhay was doing before she left for home.

'There's no cause for worry,' the nurse told her. 'He can go home.'

'Can he come to school tomorrow?'

'Maybe not tomorrow. But he should be all right by Friday. The cut in the lip was nasty but he should recover fast. You know how it is with children . . .'

Thank God. Heaving a sigh of relief she was about to leave when she saw Arundhati again near the window. But now her eyes were impossibly soft. It was clear she was standing there to have a word with Anupurba.

'Madam, are you busy?' Arundhati asked. Her tone was very sedate this time.

'No,' Anupurba said. 'Why?'

'Can I talk to you now?'

Anupurba was amazed. Silently, she took a chair on the veranda of the Health Centre and asked Arundhati to sit. She did not.

'Madam, please forgive me. I may have said something in anger . . .' Her voice failed her.

Anupurba did not speak. She looked dubiously at the person standing beside her. The thin body draped in the faded maroon salwar kameez, the lifeless features and watery eyes —everything added up to give her a pitiable appearance. What was going on inside her?

'Abhay is my son,' she said slowly, imperceptibly pausing after each word.

'Your son?' Anupurba was taken aback.

'Yes, Madam.'

Painting by Sukanya © Spastics Society of Karnataka

ten

Arundhati was the last child born to a middle-class family; both parents were aging when she arrived. Her conception had been an accident, not a desired event. There were five older siblings. By the time Arundhati entered primary school all of them were already married and her father had retired. After his retirement her only brother—the eldest of her siblings—had taken charge of the family.

He served in the police and his devotion to his work had brought him rapid promotion.

Arundhati loved her brother but feared him even more. He had brought the discipline of the police force into the home. The slightest deviation from established rules could cause an upheaval. Her old parents had given up all responsibilities and moved to the village. Arundhati's sister-in-law was good-natured but she trusted no one on earth: in-laws, relations and friends were all suspect—her husband most of all. Her lack of trust had completely destroyed her self-confidence. Her position in the home was no better than that of the domestic help. She could not take the place of Arundhati's mother.

The atmosphere within the home had become unbearable, particularly for an adolescent and so, the fourteen-year-old Arundhati frequently sought refuge with a neighbouring Christian family. While playing with their two-year-old son, John and eight-year-old daughter, Laura she forgot the problems of her own home. Rosa Aunty was very fond of her but the person Arundhati received the most affection from was Samuel Uncle, Rosa's husband. It was to him that Arundhati confided all her difficulties. Countless hours passed in conversation with him.

Two years later, the sixteen-year-old Arundhati realized that her feelings for Samuel Uncle had grown into an obsession. She could not imagine herself living apart from him.

It wasn't a one-sided relationship. Samuel was smitten too and it was at his bidding that Arundhati decided to leave home. They had a temple wedding and moved to another part of the city to live together as husband and wife.

'Temple wedding? But Samuel was Christian?' Anupurba asked in surprise. 'I thought the Christian faith doesn't allow a man to have two wives!'

'No, it doesn't,' Arundhati said. 'But I never thought of it then—I was too young to think. I trusted him blindly. I realize now that my marriage had no validity. But I swear, Madam, I married him with a pure mind, with the gods as my witness. That's why I can think of him only as my husband.'

A few days before the so-called marriage, Samuel and Arundhati moved into a tiny rented house. This news spread. Arundhati's brother almost set the house on fire when he came to know of it. He said he could have accepted Arundhati's marrying a young unmarried man of a different faith, but what she had done was unpardonable.

The decision was taken in a moment. Arundhati's brother let everyone know that for all practical purposes, she was now dead for the family. Anyone who tried to maintain any relationship with her would face banishment.

'They obeyed his command,' Arundhati said. 'Many years have passed but no one has ever come to see me. Not my mother or father—not even my sisters. As for my sister-in-law, the question does not arise.'

And what about Samuel's wife?

'If there's one person for whom my heart bleeds, it is Rosa Aunty. I know how much all this must have pained her. But what could I have done? I was totally blind,' she sighed.

Samuel was living with her but he could not give up his family either. Each day, on his way back from the office, he would visit them and inquire about their welfare. His family had come to terms with what was going on. Samuel would spend some time with them, sometimes stay for a cup of tea and then would return to Arundhati.

Three months passed like this.

Then one day this routine changed. That afternoon Samuel came first to Arundhati and told her he would have to spend the night at his other home. His daughter had typhoid.

Arundhati was left alone.

That was the beginning. After that, Samuel and Arundhati were rarely together. He spent six days out of every week with his first family and only Sundays were for Arundhati. This turn in her life left Arundhati broken, but the feeling of guilt in her mind would not allow her to protest. She could not face Rosa and the children.

Then one day Arundhati discovered that she was going to become a mother. She thought Samuel would spend more time with her now, but no such thing happened. She was confined to her home all day. But one change did come about. Her neighbours, who had referred to her contemptuously as Samuel's keep, became more supportive.

Abhay was born. The sight of that innocent face made her forget all her troubles. She had made up her mind that this child would provide the reason for her existence. She would devote the rest of her life to him.

When Abhay was seven months old, his expressions and movements raised doubts in Arundhati's mind. One day she took him to a well-known doctor. She was stunned by what he told her. Her child had cerebral palsy. He would never be normal.

'That day I died. I had endured everything—being abandoned by my own family, Samuel's neglect, everything. But this I could not take. I turned into a log of dried wood. I was sure God had punished me for robbing another person of her happiness.'

She was silent for a time. 'Slowly, all my softness vanished. I realized what was happening to me, but what could I do? My nature became harsh. And then all kinds of material desires, from some unknown source, invaded me. These days, all that I can talk to Samuel about is money and land.'

But hadn't he left her? Anupurba wondered silently.

As if she heard her, Arundhati continued, 'You must be wondering how Samuel and I are still together,' she said. 'To tell you the truth, he would surely have thrown me aside after he had had his fill of me. Most certainly after Abhay's birth. But by then the people of my neighbourhood had adopted me as their own.'

It was a harsh neighbourhood to which Samuel had moved in with Arundhati, obviously in search of an affordable home. In that locality, only the gangsters reigned. They realized her plight and became strangely protective of mother and child. They let him know how much the two were his responsibility. Samuel feared that if he abandoned Arundhati, the local goons would cut him to pieces without any hesitation and burn his house down. What Arundhati's brother had been unable to do, because of legal compunctions, would be a simple matter for them. It was out of fear that Samuel gave her some money each month and spent some time with her on Sunday evenings. Sometimes he even stayed the night.

'I searched for him desperately when the doctor told me that Abhay was spastic. After all, he was the father. I had thought he would come and tell me, "Don't worry. We'll take him to the best doctor in the world. The child will be cured." But he said nothing. There was not even the shadow of grief in his eyes. Not the slightest compassion for him. I know Abhay will never be normal; but even false sympathy would have helped.'

She sighed. After a long pause, she started talking again.

'Do you know what hurts most, Madam?' she asked. 'Abhay understands everything. Sometimes he asks me in his sign language, "Why isn't Father with us? Why doesn't he ever visit my school?" Tell me, Madam, what answer can I give him? Sometimes I wish he had been mentally retarded and not spastic.'

Tears welled up in Anupurba's eyes. Only extreme helplessness and pain can drive a mother to wish such a harsh fate for her child.

'Abhay has had surgery twice. Not once did his father come to the hospital. I had to look after everything alone. No, it wouldn't be right to say "alone". All those people, whom our society calls anti-socials and criminals, have helped me unhesitatingly, day after day. They have taken turns to sit at his bedside, forcing me to go home and bathe and rest and return.'

'Will you spend the rest of your life like this, Arundhati?' Anupurba asked. 'Haven't you ever thought of leaving Samuel?'

'I can't,' Arundhati replied. 'What other support do I have? Mrs Mathur has been kind enough to give me a job here, even though it's only temporary. I don't get paid much. How am I to manage? Still, I have hopes that with my experience, some day I will get a permanent job. Do you think I will be with Samuel after that? Several of my neighbours have suggested that I leave Samuel and find someone else. But I cannot do that. I know, even if someone does accept me, he won't accept Abhay.'

After some time she said again, 'Samuel and I bicker frequently these days. The moment I see him I tell him "Buy some land in my name. Start a fixed deposit in some bank. Buy me a house." The constant nagging and quarrels have made me harsh and rough. My nature has changed. It's humiliating to be constantly stretching out your hand for money. But let me tell you one thing, Madam, I wasn't always like this.' The helplessness in her voice had shaken Anupurba.

Slowly, Anupurba stood up. She touched Arundhati's hand but could say nothing.

'I am sorry, Madam.'

'Take care of Abhay.' That was all Anupurba could say in reply as she started walking towards her car.

Painting by P. Shishira © Spastics Society of Karnataka

eleven

The silver Mercedes 220 E Class with a uniformed chauffeur in white was rather conspicuous in their school. Who on earth could this be, Anupurba wondered, walking towards her class.

Saroja, Prachi and Ambika had all returned after their two-week training and Anupurba was now mercifully back to her earlier routine. Now she had her art classes only on Mondays and Thursdays like before. In some ways it felt rather strange to her. In some ways, she was thankful. Mrs Mathur did send her a nice handwritten letter telling her how grateful she was for the additional help. Now more children knew her and called after her, 'Anupurba Aunty, Anupurba Aunty,' as she walked past their classroom. And Anupurba, very surprisingly, had become more aware of the school and its happenings.

Maybe for that reason, she looked at the Mercedes in the parking lot again and wondered who the owner was. The person had to be some prominent personality, maybe an important business executive from a multi-national company. Sometimes dignitaries came visiting through

Shobha's efforts or at the invitation of Mrs Mathur. Some came out of a desire to help while some others just wanted to know more about the school. But one thing Anupurba had noticed: no one came unannounced. Arrangements were usually made well in advance. Some were taken to the classrooms and others to the Health Centre or the Vocational Unit. There was a process.

If it was a VIP, the visit usually ended at the Art Room —which meant that Anupurba too had to be given advance notice. But this time she had not been told. So, she wondered who the sudden visitor could be.

She decided not to speculate. It wasn't necessary for her to know everything. It could be anyone; everyone was welcome at the school.

'Madam! Madam!'

Anupurba turned around. It was Radhika. She appeared to be very excited.

'What's the matter, Radhika?'

'I've been waiting for you, Madam. Shanta Aunty is looking for you.'

'Okay, I'll go in and see her.'

Anupurba started walking towards the Principal's office.

'Madam, do you know who has come? In that big car?' Radhika said breathlessly, unable to hold back the excitement any more. The words were jostling to come out.

'No. Who?'

'It's Malini! You do not know? The film star!'

'Why is she here?'

'I don't know. There's someone with her.'

Anupurba was glad she was better informed now but really did not know who Malini was. Perhaps from the local film industry, which was big in its own right, but Anupurba was still so new to Bangalore.

Anupurba knocked on the open door to draw attention and then entered the Principal's office. Mrs Mathur looked at her in the middle of a conversation with the visitors and gestured to her to come in. Across the desk from Mrs Mathur, sat a woman in a plain salwar kameez. This must be Malini. She was pretty, but without her make-up she looked like someone you knew, not like a star or celebrity. Anupurba realized, however, that she had seen that very face many times on billboards and in newspaper ads and was aware that she was the biggest star of the local film industry until only a few years ago. With age she had graduated to playing character roles but her popularity remained undiminished. Her last three films had all been box office hits.

By her side was a gentleman with a cultured appearance and a boy who was probably fifteen or sixteen. He had a fair complexion and blue eyes. But there was no lustre in those eyes. The lips were clamped together and his face looked tense, as though he had been brought here against his will. He looked at Anupurba and looked away.

Anupurba knew that many parents who visited Asha Jyoti compelled their children to accompany them, thinking this would give them a greater sense of so-called social responsibility and probably help them become better human beings. Most did not quite realize that it did not work that way. For some children, it was an unnerving experience. Some shrivelled up within themselves. Probably, that was how the boy was feeling.

'Did you want to see me, Mrs Mathur?'

'Yes. I want you to meet Ms Malini. I am sure you know who she is. This is Anupurba.'

'Yes of course, I've seen her photographs. Hello, Ms Malini!'

'Hello!' There was that familiar smile on her face.

'This is Mr Manish, her brother, who has come from the US. And this is his son, Raja.'

'Hello,' said Manish. But Raja looked away, saying nothing.

Anupurba looked at Raja and said, 'Hi!'

Raja did not respond to Anupurba. He picked up a pencil that was lying on the desk and started drawing lines in the notebook he held in his hand.

'Raja, the lady is saying "Hi" to you!' Malini said, embarrassed.

Raja looked up from his notebook and mumbled reluctantly, 'Oh, hi!'

'Please don't mind,' Malini said again. 'Our Raja has his moods. When he feels like it he talks so much it's difficult to make him stop. But if he's not in the mood you just can't get a word out of him.'

Anupurba was feeling uneasy. Why say such things about the child in his presence? Although Anupurba had taught only in an elementary school she had come across many teenagers, both here and in America. She had always noticed one thing: adolescent children did not like adults discussing their behaviour with strangers.

But Malini had not finished. 'Raja was not always like this,' she went on. 'It's only in the last four or five months that he has become so moody. My brother has tried many things—counselling, psychiatric treatment and what not. You know, in the US all these are easy to access; but nothing seems to have worked.'

Stop it please! Couldn't she see that all this was making things more difficult for the child?

Malini noticed the uneasiness in Anupurba's eyes. With a careless gesture of her hand she said, 'Don't worry! I don't think he has heard a word of what we have been saying. He has a problem.'

How easily she said the word! Anupurba was shocked.

Mrs Mathur interjected, 'Raja has been admitted to the eighth standard in our school today. We don't usually admit children at the close of the year, but Raja is different. He is very talented.'

Anupurba's eyes turned back to Raja. Did that mean he had cerebral palsy? She felt a churning inside her. Externally, there was absolutely nothing abnormal about the child, neither in his speech nor in his physical appearance. Then her eyes took in the child's feet. The shoe on his left foot was normal, but the one on the right was designed differently.

'Anupurba, I sent for you for two reasons,' Mrs Mathur said. 'Firstly, because of Raja's language problem.'

'Language? His English seemed perfect.'

'I mean, his American accent,' Mrs Mathur explained. 'Raja was born in the US and has been raised there, so he speaks English the American way. I found it difficult to follow what he was saying, so I expect it will be even more difficult for the others. But I'm sure you'll have no problems.'

'No, none at all.'

'In that case, can I make a request? Could you meet the eighth standard in the morning tomorrow? I have spoken to Prachi, our eighth standard class teacher. There aren't too many children in her class, so Raja's arrival won't be a problem. At the same time, it's the end of the year. Prachi will have to find out from Raja what he has learnt in his previous school. But the problem is with our ability to understand his accent. Prachi can't follow him easily. It's not exactly a big deal but it takes up a lot of time before she gets it. It can be difficult for a teacher to devote so much time to one child. But if you're there to help, it's another matter. Can you come tomorrow, Anupurba? Please—just for a couple of hours? Just tomorrow.'

'Certainly, Mrs Mathur, and not just for a couple of hours. I'll be with Prachi the whole day and come on Wednesday too if necessary. You'll see, there'll be no problems after a day or two. He will be fine.'

Mrs Mathur looked at Anupurba and smiled, as though she had always known this was the answer she would get. 'There's something else I wanted to show you,' she said.

She extended the large yellow file that lay on her desk towards Anupurba. 'Raja loves to draw. These are some of his drawings.'

Anupurba was stunned by what she saw. Never in all her years as an art teacher had she seen such talent in a child—not here in Asha Jyoti or for that matter in the US. Could this be the work of a fifteen-year-old? How incredible!

'These are unbelievably good!'

'Thanks!' This one was from Raja.

His eyes were not on Anupurba but his ears were alert. He had been listening to every word said about his drawing. That surely meant that he had heard all that his aunt had previously been saying about him. Oh God!

Malini was preparing to leave. 'Thanks, Mrs Mathur,' she said. 'I'll go now. Raja will start coming here tomorrow. Please take care for the first few days.' The beautiful eyes showed so much apprehension.

Before Mrs Mathur could say anything, Manish stood up. 'Malini,' he said, 'I'd like to have a quick look at the Art Room and see the children's drawings. Can you please wait here for a few minutes with Raja? . . . Do you mind?' he asked, turning to Anupurba.

'Not at all,' she said. 'Please come.'

They reached the Art Room and Anupurba was about to take the children's drawings out of the cupboard when Manish stopped her. 'I didn't really want to see the drawings,' he said, 'but there is something I had to tell you.'

'Please!' she said, gesturing him to take a chair.

'I know you didn't like what Malini said. But please don't mind. She's so concerned about Raja that sometimes she forgets herself. Raja doesn't have a mother. Malini has given him a mother's love since he was a small child.'

So Raja did not have a mother. Anupurba looked at Manish sympathetically.

'No, it is not what you are thinking. Raja's mother is alive. . . . Actually, we are divorced. Eileen's American. We studied together at the university. She came to India for the first time after we were married. That was her first exposure to family life in India and she didn't quite like what she saw. She felt we Indians interfere too much in the lives of others, including our own children. And husbands didn't allow their wives any space.'

Not entirely untrue. Anupurba was listening.

'The problem grew worse after Raja was born. When we found that the child was slow in a few activities, we took him to many doctors. They all said the same thing—mild form of cerebral palsy. It may not be a major hindrance in life, but it would always be there in him, and it was incurable.'

'From that day Eileen started feeling suffocated. She felt as though she had suddenly been made a prisoner and was being punished for some unknown crime. Her wings had been clipped. One day she asked me to send Raja to some institution, no matter what the cost. Money wasn't our problem, but I couldn't do it. I couldn't think of entrusting Raja to someone else's care. Eileen was exasperated with me. If parents could send children to boarding schools and parents to old-age homes, what was the problem in sending a child with cerebral palsy to an institution that would look after him well for the rest of his life? The arguments and the bitterness grew, and finally, she and I divorced. Eileen migrated to Australia. She has visited America several times since but never cared to inquire about Raja or look him up.'

And then?

'After a lot of thinking, I had a discussion with Malini and then I had Raja admitted to a school when he was a little older. But it was a school for normal children.'

'A normal school? Why?'

'That isn't an easy question to answer. A father's mind, you know. It isn't always easy to confront the reality. I convinced myself that apart from a slight limp, Raja showed none of the symptoms of cerebral palsy. Why should I have made a fuss over something ao minor? To tell you the truth, I didn't want people to know. No one knew, apart from Malini and Eileen—not even my closest friends. I thought what he needed was to see other kids, learn from them, even get competitive.'

Anupurba was listening silently.

'It's true that Raja was a slow learner. He found his lessons difficult and had some trouble in learning how to write—that's why he's still in the eighth grade at sixteen. But I told myself, not all children are born brilliant. So what if his grades are low? Let him get through high school somehow. I tried to hide his problems from others, giving it out as attention deficit disorder. I realize now that this was a mistake. I should have known that Raja was not normal, though he looked normal. I should have sent him to a special school. He might have been different if he had been given therapy and special education and allowed to interact with others like him.'

'Why, what happened?'

'In the process of my trying to make him normal, he was hurt emotionally. I don't know if he'll ever be able to get over it.' His voice choked.

Then, controlling his feelings, he continued, 'You know what schools in America are like: adolescent children have boyfriends and girlfriends. With his mental condition, Raja could not have developed more than an ordinary friendship with any girl. But there was peer pressure and he kept trying. Finally, when he was in the eighth grade, he became close to Jenny, who was a year junior to him. Shortly afterwards, the eighth grade children organized a dance. Raja wasn't keen to go—what could he have done at a dance with his lame leg? But Jenny persuaded him to go. She couldn't go to the dance if she wasn't escorted by an eighth grade student.'

'Did Raja take Jenny to the dance?'

'Yes. But once she was inside, she danced merrily with everyone else. Once, during the dance, Raja asked her to sit beside him. "Why?" Jenny asked. "Just because you can't dance?" "You are my girlfriend." Raja said to her. "Girlfriend? You must be out of your mind!" she told him.

'Raja was badly hurt by this incident and went into a depression. He wouldn't speak to anyone. Then I took him to a number of psychiatrists. They all told me the same thing: I had made a mistake in sending him to a normal school. Raja's mental condition was so shattered then that the Principal of the school asked me to come over for a chat. I realized I could no longer hide the truth. But once the facts were known, who could guarantee that Raja wouldn't have to face all kinds of taunts? I couldn't stay on in the US and returned to India. Ten days ago I came to Bangalore. I have come to terms with reality. I am very hopeful that Raja can improve at Asha Jyoti.'

'I'm sure, he will,' Anupurba assured him. 'I'll look after him myself.'

'Thank you so very much. I feel relieved that I have told you everything. Bye, Mrs Anupurba.'

'Please, just call me Anupurba,' was all she said in reply as they shook hands and he got up to go.

Painting by Jhansi © Spastics Society of Karnataka

twelve

Anupurba's assurance was not misplaced. As February gave way to March and the pink and the yellow tabebuia bloomed in abundance, Raja settled down in his new school happily.

He had made friends very quickly. Despite a broken home behind him, Raja was very affectionate by nature. Moreover, unlike the school in the US, no one at Asha Jyoti singled him out for not being 'normal'. No one even thought that he had a disability. He was not even given a furtive second look. Having a disability was the normal thing here!

There was another reason why he found easy acceptance—it was his amazing artistic talent. All that the boy needed was drawing material and the way he created magic with pencil and paper amazed everyone. On the very first day, he drew a sketch of Varun who had dozed off during the class. Varun's mouth was gaping open with a little drool by the side. The other children had never seen such a life-like sketch before! They were in fits of laughter. Neither Prachi nor Anupurba were able to calm them down. Raja's drawing had brought them so much of joy. Finally, one of the other children, unable to restrain herself, woke up Varun. Varun pretended to be angry for a brief moment when he saw the object of the collective amusement, but soon he too burst out laughing. It really was a marvellous drawing.

'Okay, that's enough!' Prachi tried to bring everyone back to focus on their work at last, but muffled chuckles went on for a long time. Raja just blended into the place as if he had always been a part of this school, these people.

The only occasional stumbling block was his accent and sometimes his choice of words.

'These guys are wonderful!' Raja told Anupurba later that day. 'Never seen anybody like them! But why can't anyone understand me? Should I do something differently?'

Before Anupurba could say anything Shweta walked up to them. Since she was in Anupurba's art class, she felt comfortable with her. Pushing her long curly hair back, she said, as though trying to probe a secret, 'Anupurba Aunty, we were asking Raja about his school in America and he said "I love the dance, I love the dance". What is he saying?'

Anupurba was startled. Dance! Could Raja be telling his new friends about the sordid saga of his school dance? Was the story of his humiliation surfacing all over again? Should she know?

'What was it, Raja, what were you telling Shweta?' she asked gently.

'Oh, Mrs Anu, they asked me what I liked best in my

school in the US and I told them. But they don't understand.'

'Well, what was it you liked the most?'

'We had a big pond near the school. There were little stones at the bottom and there were a lot of ducks. I used to sit on a bench beside the pool and I loved the ducks. They built their nest in spring and hatched little ducklings this time of the year there . . .'

Now Anupurba could understand what had happened. Raja had been talking about 'ducks' in his slightly nasal American accent and the children had understood him to be saying 'dance'.

Smiling, she explained to Shweta in her teacher voice 'Raja was talking about "ducks", not "dance". You can see lots of them in the US; they are beautiful, with their brown, green and yellow colours. There was a pond in Raja's old school, where ducks built their nests. They laid their eggs in the bushes near the banks. Little chicks came out of the eggs. This was what Raja was trying to tell you.'

She turned to Raja. 'Raja, you should speak very slowly to your friends so that they can follow you.'

He nodded.

By the end of the day, she found that the children were no longer struggling to communicate with Raja, though they had to listen to him intently. Good. Her work was done. They had broken the ice. She probably needn't come and sit in Prachi's class any longer. As she was leaving, she remembered something. 'Come to my art class tomorrow, Raja. We must show your drawings at the exhibition.'

'Art class? I don't know anything about it,' he said.

'Shweta will bring you there. She's in the same class.'

'That's great, thank you so much.'

~

The Art Exhibition was barely five weeks away. Shobha had already fixed the dates in consultation with Mrs Mathur—April 15,16 and 17. The Arts Council of Karnataka had granted them permission to exhibit their paintings in the large hall without a fee. Everything depended on Anupurba now.

It was a tremendous responsibility. They were all banking on her. Could she pull it off?

On Thursday Raja turned up at the art class accompanied by Shweta.

Another new class. New children. Raja observed everyone for a moment and then, for some unexplainable reason, withdrew into his shell. The atmosphere here was different from his classroom as there were children of different ages, drawn from different classes. Raja was uneasy.

But Anupurba did not have to make an effort to put him at ease—Shweta did it for her. Garrulous Shweta never stopped chattering or giggling in the art class; she was always up to something. Anupurba largely ignored her antics. Sometimes she would abandon her own drawing and start helping the younger children with their work or she would knot their hair ribbons into flowers of different shapes or go and ask the children intent on their own drawings what they were up to even as her own work lagged behind. Now Shweta had found something else to keep her busy—Raja. Her efforts to make him feel at ease bore fruit. On other days Anupurba would have been irritated by Shweta's lack of concentration, but today she welcomed it. She was Raja's companion, his comfort factor across continents and cultures in an unfamiliar world which was now going to be his.

~

The art lessons went on. Two weeks had gone by since Raja's arrival. Now he was like any one else at Asha Jyoti. His occasional American accent gave the children innocent amusement. But Raja was unperturbed. He had realized by now that there was no malice behind the jokes and the laughter at his drawl.

'Look Anupurba Aunty, Raja is pulling my hair.'

Anupurba looked up from her work.

'What are you doing, Raja?' she said, a little firmly.

She had never seen him doing anything mischievous before. Was he picking up the wrong habits from Shweta?

'Nothing, Aunty.'

He let go of Shweta's hair and became quiet. His face turned red. It had taken him a long time to address his teachers as Aunty. Like all American children he had persisted in calling them Mr, Mrs, but now that had finally changed.

'What do you mean by "nothing"?' She was serious. 'I saw you pull Shweta's hair myself.'

Raja said nothing. He sat with his head bowed. There was a triumphant smile on Shweta's lips.

Srinivas spoke up. 'It isn't Raja's fault, Aunty. Shweta wasn't letting him draw. She was spreading her hair all over the paper.'

Anupurba suppressed her laughter with difficulty. Feigning anger, she said, 'Shweta, I'll have to punish you if you do it again. It's not nice to disturb others in the classroom.'

'Please, Anupurba Aunty,' Raja said with sudden anxiety, 'it's okay. Shweta wasn't doing it on purpose.'

'Hm!' Anupurba said. 'Very well, Shweta, I'll excuse you this time. But if I see you doing it again, I'll send you back to your own class. No art class for you!'

With her head lowered, Shweta picked up a pencil in her crooked fingers and busied herself in drawing.

What a child this Shweta was!

Anyone who took one look at Shweta could have guessed that she was suffering from some serious physical or mental disability. She had thin, pinched features. Her hands and legs were disproportionately tiny. Each one of her fingers and toes were crooked. Elongated face. Flat nose. Round eyes. Nothing was attractive about her, except her hair. The long curly locks fell in waves across her back. Her mother would sometimes insist on braiding her hair when she sent her to school, but the moment Shweta arrived she would pull out the ribbons with her crooked fingers and release her hair again. It was very clear how much she loved her tresses.

The class ended. The children emerged from the room

noisily. Unobtrusively, Anupurba observed Shweta from behind. Today she was dressed in a salwar kameez. Her arms were covered by the long, blue dupatta. The salwar extended to her feet. The deformity of her limbs was concealed. What dominated her presence was her curly hair, reaching down to her waist.

She had glorious hair! Like a supermodel in a shampoo ad. Only, Shweta would never become a model. But she knew this was her most beautiful feature, as beautiful as it got in the world of beautiful people.

Shweta might have become aware that Anupurba's eyes were on her. She suddenly turned her head around, looked at Anupurba and broke into a dazzling smile. What beauty, what innocence there was in that smile!

Anupurba couldn't help but think: What future did the Shwetas of this world have?

Not just today—that thought crossed her mind all the time, particularly as she watched the young adults among the children who were standing on the threshold of the springtime of their lives.

She sometimes brought up this issue with her husband when they sat drinking tea together on a Sunday afternoon. 'Tell me, Amrit, do these children have a future? They may have parents or grandparents now, but will they always be around to take care of them? How will they manage if they out-live them? Who will look after them?'

She knew her husband had no answer but that didn't stop her from asking.

She had asked many others at Asha Jyoti the same question.

Shobha would raise her hands heavenwards and say, 'Who are we, Purba? Surely the same Creator who has brought them into this world will look after them. I believe they are children of God, hopefully a better God than the one who looks after us.'

But Bani was more pragmatic. 'Many of these children have a short life-span, Anupurba. In some ways, that is probably a better thing. Moreover, it makes no sense for us to worry about their future; their present is gloomy enough. Each moment is so painful, even for those who are able to get a lot of care. If the suffering isn't physical, it's mental.'

All very true, but so difficult to accept.

Anupurba raised the same topic when she was with Ranjana later that day. After a brief silence, Ranjana had said philosophically, 'Future? Does anyone know the future? But then, things aren't entirely hopeless, are they? Look at our Radhika. Or Noor. They are carrying on.'

'Yes, but it's a familiar world in which they are living. There's a bigger world beyond this.'

'Yes, there is. Several of them have slowly set foot on that as well—several of the children of our own school. Raghav is a graphic designer now. Sharbari is a receptionist in an office. Jayita is a Customer Relations Officer in a company . . .'

Ranjana might have named others but Anupurba interjected. 'But what about their personal lives? Can they ever find a companion? And you've told me yourself that they have all the same desires and aversions as normal people.'

Ranjana looked directly at Anupurba's face. In a low voice, she said, 'Let me tell you something, Anupurba. What you just mentioned is true. Spastic children have the same wants as ordinary children. The same hunger, thirst, fear. And more.'

'Meaning?'

'Even the same sexual desires. They have healthy minds. How can they not want physical companionship? But they . . .'

She was unable to continue.

Anupurba's eyes were wet too.

'You know, we provide them sex education when they grow up. We do it differently from the way it's done in other schools. Here we tell them to take care of their desires; we teach them that masturbation is no sin.'

Anupurba could take it no more. 'I have to go. Tons of things to do,' she said as she hurried out of the door.

She might have said the words to put an end to the disturbing conversation, but it was a fact that she needed to reach home on time. Their close friends from the US, Sudha and Arun, were to arrive on Friday evening. Jeet and Bobby had been close to their two children since they were very young. They were all coming to spend two days with them and then fly to Kerala on Monday for a vacation. Anupurba was looking forward to their arrival.

~

Anupurba felt unusually cheerful and happy as she drove to Asha Jyoti on Monday afternoon. But once in class, her joy vanished.

The garrulous Shweta was totally quiet today. She wore a thick cotton scarf tied round her head. Prabha, who was sitting on Shweta's right, was repeatedly asking her something. No response from Shweta. Raja, on her left, was also questioning her in a low voice, with an anxious look in his eyes. Shweta was quiet.

'What happened, Shweta?' Prabha said in a loud voice suddenly, sounding irritated. 'Can't you answer my question?'

Shweta opened her mouth at last. 'I don't want to talk to anyone,' she said.

'Why?' The ten-year-old Prabha wouldn't give up.

'My wish!'

'Very well, don't talk if you don't want to, but let me braid your hair.' Prabha pulled the black scarf off Shweta's head before she could say anything. And in the very next moment, not only she, but the rest of the class, seemed to turn into stone.

Shweta's long curly hair was gone. It had been cropped short. Rather awkwardly at that.

Shweta burst into sobs. The class looked on in silence. Before Anupurba could speak, Raja had left his chair and moved to her side. Tying the black scarf back tenderly round Shweta's head, he said, 'It's okay, it's okay. It's just your hair—it will grow again soon. Nothing to worry. Don't cry, Shweta! Your hair will grow back in six months.'

'Will it really, Raja?' Shweta said, weeping.

'It will, I promise you! You'll see!'

'I don't know why my mother got annoyed with me,' Shweta said. 'I hadn't done anything. My younger brother was sleeping and I just spread my hair over his face. I was playing with him. He got frightened and started crying. But I didn't want to frighten him. Why did my mother get so angry?'

Raja did not know either Shweta's mother or her younger brother; but still, he stroked her arm softly and said, 'I'm sure she isn't angry. All right, tell me who tied that scarf round your head?'

'My mother.'

'You see! Would she do that if she was angry? Maybe she was frightened too! But she loves you. That's why she tied the scarf round your head!'

An irrefutable argument.

Shweta stopped sobbing at last.

'My mother isn't angry?'

'No, not at all. She loves you,' he repeated.

'And my hair will grow again?'

'Yes'

Shweta smiled.

Raja went back to his place.

Prabha, who had been watching the scene nervously, suddenly clutched Shweta's hand. 'I'm sorry, Shweta,' she said.

'It's all right.' Once again she was her old self. 'Raja said my hair will grow back in six months. Now it will be even nicer than before. Then you can braid my hair.

Anupurba Aunty, I have heard that hair becomes thicker when it is cut, is that true?'

Anupurba had been reduced to silence by the entire episode. She was startled by her question.

'Yes, it will become even more beautiful than before, Shweta. You'll see!'

Shweta went back to her drawing.

Anupurba was lost in thought. She looked at the profusion of Bangalore's spring flowers outside the window of her class, and the faces of the children appeared in her mind's eye and seemed to be reflected in them.

Painting by Arun Cherian © Spastics Society of Karnataka

thirteen

There were still a few minutes before the end of the class when Shobha came rushing into the Art Room.

'Purba, do you have some time to spare after the class? Can you come out with me for an hour or two?'

'Why, what's the matter?' Anupurba was alarmed.

'I'll tell you later. Come to the reception when your class gets over. I'll be waiting for you.'

After the class, Anupurba closed the cupboard full of paintings and went to the reception. Shobha was already there, waiting for her impatiently. She looked worried. She was running her eyes over some papers but they seemed to take in nothing.

'Shobha!'

'Oh, you are here. Let's go. Can we use your car?'

'Yes, of course. But where are we going?'

'I will tell you in a moment.' Shobha was not her usual self.

As soon as they got into the car, Shobha asked Somashekhar to drive to an apartment block on Cunningham Road.

Cunningham Road? So far away from the school? Why were they going there?

'What's the matter, Shobha? Where are we going?' Anupurba asked again.

After a moment's silence Shobha said, 'I met Shubhendu today, Purba.'

'Shubhendu!' She had never thought she would hear that name again. 'Is he in Bangalore?'

'It seems he's been here for the last eight years. And neither of us knew of the other's presence.' Her voice was muffled. She was looking through the window vacantly.

The past began to unfold before Anupurba's eyes: Shobha and Shubhendu standing in front of the library for hours, chatting; arguing noisily about some character in a novel; lamenting the corruption that had gripped the country, wanting to change the world.

They had all been amazed. How could someone as handsome and brilliant as Shubhendu fall for a plain, straight-talking girl like Shobha? And this wasn't the light-hearted romance of college life, but the serious commitment of two people who planned to spend the rest of their lives together. 'Opposites attract,' some said. Shobha wasn't a brilliant student. Nor was she a great beauty. But she had the freshness of youth and an unusual, fiery spirit that made her different from others.

'Reena is very ill,' Shobha suddenly said.

Anupurba stared at her. Reena's name on Shobha's lips!

Reena was their classmate. But she had been quite

different from them. She was the only daughter of a wealthy business family—the first girl in three generations. She was pampered. She only had to make a wish and everyone would jump to fulfil it—father, uncles, brothers, everyone. Her older brother chauffeured her to college every morning and her younger uncle drove her back. The family kitchen catered exclusively to her tastes. When they vacationed, it was she who chose the place; when she went shopping with her mother or aunts it was never a single sari or one dress; it was always a pile of clothes. She rarely wore a dress twice. Anupurba had witnessed all of this.

Dazzling beauty that she was, Reena need not have gone to such pains to attract people, but when she came to college she was like an enchantress, casting a spell on the whole world.

Then one day she wished to possess Shubhendu.

Shobha's Shubhendu.

Was it possible that Reena could want something and not get it? Anupurba never knew how it happened and nor did her friends, but one day Shubhendu, the best student of the MA Political Science class, broke off all relations with Shobha of the English Honours class.

And soon they learnt that he had a new love—Reena.

The BA examinations ended soon afterwards and Shobha moved to Delhi to do her Master's degree in Sociology. Anupurba's father was transferred to Berhampur and she moved there with the family. She took admission for an MA degree in English Literature from Berhampur University. Life moved on.

Then one day when she was in the final year, she received a wedding invitation. Shubhendu was getting married to Reena. She had torn up the card in anger and disgust. Since that day she had heard nothing of either Shubhendu or Reena.

'How did you get to know that Shubhendu was here?' she asked slowly.

'I didn't know,' Shobha said haltingly. 'For the last two or three years Asha Jyoti has been receiving cheques regularly from R.S. Industries. Not huge amounts, but not too small either. Although Mrs Mathur has been communicating her thanks to their Chairman over the telephone, I thought I must visit them at least once in person. I couldn't find the time earlier, but finally I made an appointment and went there this morning. And I found the company's Chairman was . . .' Her voice trailed off.

Anupurba was amazed. 'Shubhendu?'

Shobha silently nodded.

'He looks so different now,' Shobha said. 'Though he hasn't put on weight, his hair has thinned a lot and there are dark circles below his eyes. But then we all have changed a lot too. You couldn't recognize me at the Art Exhibition the other day, could you? But Shubhendu recognized me at once.'

'What about you?'

Shobha smiled dryly. There was a time when she could recognize even his footsteps.

'And then?' Anupurba asked.

'He told me all about himself as we talked.'

'What was there to tell? Don't we know everything?'

Anupurba was bitter.

Shobha sighed. 'Why rake up the old story?'

'Quite right. Eighteen years is a long time.'

'He married Reena after he got into the civil services,' Shobha said haltingly.

'I know.'

'You do?'

'Yes, I received the wedding invitation when I was in my final year.'

'Oh. After he had served in various places for a few years, he quit to set up his own business at his in-laws' insistence and Reena's wish. Eventually they shifted to Bangalore. Reena had grown to like the city. And it was here that their first child was born, eight years after their marriage. A son. But he was a spastic.'

'Spastic! Oh my God!'

Who could imagine that such a thing could ever happen in Reena's life!

'Yes. Reena nearly went mad. So did Shubhendu. They took the child to the US. Then they had him admitted to a hospital in Germany, where he remained for a long time. But it didn't do any good. They were forced to come back to India. That was when Reena had her first nervous breakdown. She was convinced that someone was using black magic to destroy her life.'

Black magic! Anupurba could not imagine Reena being capable of such thoughts.

'Someone must have planted the idea in her mind. Everyone in her parent's home was concerned. They consulted numerous doctors. Finally, their family physician advised them that Reena could become normal if she had another child.'

'Did she have another child?'

'Yes, she had a son a year ago. But this child too has cerebral palsy.'

'What are you saying?' Anupurba cried out.

Only a moment ago she had been cursing Reena mentally. But what could be a greater curse than the life she must be living?

'Her entire world is shattered. She had a second nervous breakdown a few months ago. And now, Shubhendu told me, she does nothing all day but keep watch over her two children like a hawk. There are trained nurses to look after them but she won't trust anyone. She won't sleep at night. She refuses to take any medicines for fear she might drop off to sleep, leaving her children unprotected. Her mental condition is getting worse by the day. Who knows what will happen if things go on like this?'

'Why don't they send the children to Asha Jyoti? The older child must be old enough to go to school.'

'That's why we are going there now, Purba,' Shobha said. 'To see Reena and Shubhendu. He thinks she may agree if we—I explain things to her.'

'You? You are to explain things to Reena? How could he make such a request to you?'

'Shubhendu's request was to a professional in Asha Jyoti and not to any particular individual. How could I have refused?'

After a brief silence she said, 'I did agree when

Shubhendu spoke to me, but when I was returning to Asha Jyoti I had doubts. I didn't have the courage. I couldn't have asked anyone else to accompany me, but you know everything, and so . . .'

~

Cunningham Road was in the prosperous part of Bangalore. Fairly old, and close to the Cantonment Railway Station, it must have gotten its name from the British. Where old colonial bungalows once stood on an acre or so of land, apartment complexes had now come up. Anupurba and Shobha stopped at the gate of one such apartment complex. From the outside, there was no sign of opulence. But inside, it was like a five-star hotel. A big marble lobby with a fountain in the middle, stairs of black granite and the expensive chandelier made it obvious that only the very rich lived here.

'Which apartment, Madam?'

Shobha told the guard the number.

'What is your name, Madam?'

'Shobha,' she replied mechanically.

The man dialled a number on the intercom and after a couple of rings, spoke.

'Shobha Madam to visit you, Sir. Okay, Sir. Yes, I'll send them up. Thank you, Sir.'

Sir. Shubhendu was obviously at home.

Anupurba had regarded Shubhendu with curiosity when she was in college, especially after she had come to know of his relationship with Shobha. But she had hardly known him. Should she descend on him unannounced? There was nothing wrong in it, she told herself. She too was a representative of Asha Jyoti.

The security guard led them to the lift, respectfully holding the door open.

As she pressed the button marked '3', Anupurba realized that there were only six apartments in this enormous residential complex. You couldn't expect someone like Reena to be cooped up in a pigeon hole, could you? Her family would never have allowed it.

Anupurba checked herself suddenly. Why was she so bitter? If Shobha could forgive Shubhendu and Reena, why was she, merely a spectator, so unforgiving?

She told herself to become calm.

The door was open when the two got off the elevator and Shubhendu himself was there to greet them.

'This is Anupurba, she teaches at Asha Jyoti. You may not remember her but she was in our college.'

'Hello,' said Shubhendu, 'Please come inside.'

Thank God, it wasn't anything more than that. And why should it be any other way? Anupurba suddenly lost all her discomfiture and regarded it simply as a social worker's visit. Her knowledge of the past was irrelevant.

As the two stepped in, Shubhendu told them that he would take them rightaway to his wife's room. For a fleeting moment, Anupurba felt a twinge of anxiety about meeting a neurotic woman. But the next moment, they were face to face with Reena.

Shubhendu announced, 'These ladies are from Asha

Jyoti. I told you about Asha Jyoti, didn't I? The cerebral palsy school.'

Reena looked at them with narrow, distrustful eyes for a while. Then she said in a voice devoid of all emotion, 'You are Shobha. And you are Anupurba, aren't you?'

'How are you, Reena?' Anupurba asked. Shobha said nothing.

'Why have you come here?' Reena said.

Shubhendu was embarrassed. He said, almost in a whisper, 'They have come from Asha Jyoti. I asked them to come. For Tito and Luna.'

'For Tito and Luna? Why Tito and Luna?' Her voice was bitter.

Shobha seated herself on the sofa next to Reena. 'Shubhendu told us that Tito isn't going to school yet,' she said gently. 'Luna is too young to go to school, but Tito should be going, shouldn't he?'

'Why?' Reena was confrontational.

'He's eight years old now.'

'So? Why does he need to go to school? Is he going to get a job? Or look after his parents?' There was sarcasm in her voice.

'That's not the only reason for sending a child to school. There's so much to learn.'

'That's enough. Have you come here to give me advice?'

'Why should I do that?'

'Why else would you say such things? About a child like Tito? Don't you know he's incapable of learning anything?'

'Who told you that, Reena? Shubhendu has told me everything. Tito has cerebral palsy. That means he has a physical problem for sure, but maybe there is nothing wrong with his brain. He can learn things at school, like many other children. It will take time, but it's possible. Besides, we don't just make children study at Asha Jyoti. We give them many different kinds of education. We give them therapy. Counselling. Soon there will be vocational training as well. Tito may even become self-reliant if he goes to Asha Jyoti for a few years.'

'Self-reliant! He doesn't need to be self-reliant as long as I am alive,' Reena almost shouted.

'And if you are not? God forbid, but what if something happens to you? Who will look after Tito?'

'You are a real well-wisher, aren't you?' Reena put down the child she was holding in her lap on the sofa and jumped up in anger. 'You are planning to kill me! I know all your tricks, Shobha. You think I snatched Shubhendu away from you, so now you want to rob me of my child. But I won't let you!' She clutched the child desperately to her bosom. The child, rudely shaken awake, began to cry.

Shobha's face flushed red with humiliation and shame.

Shubhendu too was shocked. 'Calm down, Reena,' he said in embarrassment and helpless anger.

Neither Shobha nor Shubhendu could calm Reena down. Finally, Anupurba spoke.

'No one can help you if you are determined to be unreasonable, Reena.'

'I don't need anyone's help,' Reena said. 'I'm just fine the way I am. Be quiet, Luna, my love, my darling.' She suddenly burst into tears as she was caressing her child.

Shobha sat down beside her again.

'Forget everything that's past, Reena. But do come once to Asha Jyoti with your children. See everything for yourself. If you like what you see, you can send Tito to our school, but if you decide otherwise, that's fine.'

Reena said nothing.

Shubhendu said, 'Tito has fever now. We'll bring him to Asha Jyoti when he is better.'

Again Reena said nothing. Did it mean that she was giving in although she wasn't particularly happy about it? Somehow, Anupurba knew it was not so. This was clearly a futile visit.

Shobha stood up. It was time to leave. Anupurba followed her.

'What's this, are you leaving?' Shubhendu said. 'Won't you have a cup of tea?'

'Sorry, we have to go. Purba's children must have returned from school by now. Another time maybe.'

Shubhendu did not insist.

'Let me escort you downstairs then,' Shubhendu said.

'Please don't bother,' Shobha said emphatically.

As the elevator door closed Anupurba could sense a storm rising inside Shobha.

Once she was inside the car, Shobha allowed her tears to flow. Somashekhar could see her in the rear-view mirror, but she didn't care. She had kept the tension bottled up inside for decades now. It needed release.

Anupurba held her hand. The two friends did not speak for the rest of the journey.

Painting by Hemlatha © Spastics Society of Karnataka

fourteen

The police had detained all cars for more than forty minutes to allow a procession to pass. Anupurba looked at her watch exasperatedly a few times and finally gave up. She was going to be horribly late today. The lunch break would have ended by now.

She had, of course, called Ranjana on her cell phone and informed her. The airport road traffic was simply not moving and there was nothing she could do. Finally, when the cars ahead of her started moving a little, she had already lost a lot of time.

Moving slowly through the jam, Somashekhar finally managed to get her to the school gate. As she got out of the car hurriedly and started walking towards the school building, Anupurba saw a lady getting out of an auto-rickshaw. She wore a green nylon sari and had a cheap black purse slung from her shoulder. She looked to be in her mid-forties.

'Excuse me . . .'

Anupurba stopped.

'Do you work in this school?'

No, she didn't work there; she was a volunteer; she took some art classes for now. All this would have taken too long to explain, so she merely said, 'Yes, are you looking for something?'

'I have to meet someone in the school but I don't know how.'

'Please go that way, you'll find the reception desk in the corridor. Please ask the receptionist and she will help you. Whom do you want to see?'

'Arundhati Ramchandran,' the lady said, hesitating. She seemed to pause after every syllable.

Arundhati?

She had said she had no friends or relatives. Who was this lady then? A neighbour? Then why had she come to the school looking for Arundhati?

Well, she had no time to think about it now.

'Come with me. I'll take you to the reception.' Anupurba and the visitor walked up to where Radhika was. Radhika was busy organizing all the morning newspapers neatly. She looked in complete possession of her space.

'Radhika!'

'Yes, Madam?'

'This lady wants to meet Arundhati. Can you please help her?'

With that brief handover, as she was walking towards the Art Room, Anupurba heard Radhika say 'She's not here, Madam. One of the children in her class was taken ill suddenly and Arundhati Didi had to take her to the

Health Centre. She won't be back for at least an hour. You can wait here.'

~

The class ended with the usual growing excitement—the children did not have the faintest idea about what the exhibition would be like! They had never done this before. It was amazing how the process of preparation had touched them so intensely. It seemed as if they were all experiencing a sense of flow. Anupurba lovingly took stock of the day's harvest, locked all the paintings in the cupboard, wished the cacophonous children goodbye and walked out of the classroom. As she neared the reception, she was surprised to see the same lady still waiting.

So Arundhati hadn't returned yet?

She walked up to Radhika. 'Radhika, hasn't Arundhati come back?'

'No ma'am. I had called up the Health Centre. The child in Room 7 who had had a fall needs some stitches in her head. Her parents hadn't come and Arundhati Didi was unable to leave the child alone. But I guess she must be on her way now. . . . Oh, there she is! Arundhati Didi, there's someone waiting to see you.'

'See you, Radhika. Bye, Arundhati.' Anupurba started walking out with a wave.

'Bye, ma'am.' It was Radhika. But there was no response from Arundhati.

By then, she had already seen the visitor and had become stiff.

'Arundhati,' the lady said, rising.

'Why have you come here?' There was umbrage in Arundhati's voice.

'I wanted to speak to you, Arundhati.' The lady almost implored.

'But I have nothing to say to you,' Arundhati said firmly and began to walk away. She did not care that there were two other people watching the interaction curiously.

'Please Arundhati, don't go away!'

'Tell me quickly whatever you have to say.' Arundhati stopped. Her voice was severe.

'Please . . .'

Anupurba did not mean to eavesdrop on the conversation that followed but she could not help picking up a few words here and there.

Flat . . . Samuel . . . the children . . .

Suddenly she heard Arundhati raise her voice. 'Why are you doing all this? Didn't I tell you over the phone once and for all that I was sorry for what had happened? But is it all *my* fault? I am doing what I can, but why are you poking your nose into this?'

The woman said something to Arundhati in a low pleading voice.

'Please go away. Leave me to fight my own battles.'

Now it was the other woman's voice that could be heard. The same pleading voice. 'Arundhati, I know how you are suffering. But what crime have we three committed against you? What is happening now is making life unbearable, not just for me but for the children as well. Don't think of me if you don't want to, but please think of John and Laura.'

Anupurba stopped in her stride. John and Laura. Hadn't she heard these names before? Where? Weren't these the names of Samuel's two children? Then was this woman Samuel's wife? Rosa? Why was she here?

Two ayahs stood nearby, listening inquisitively to the war of words between Arundhati and the visitor. Radhika was also staring at them in surprise.

Anupurba couldn't restrain herself from intervening.

'Arundhati, if it's some personal matter you are discussing, you can use the Art Room. There's no one there now.'

'No, there's nothing to discuss, Madam.'

Arundhati turned round to face the other woman and said with a sudden finality, 'Please go. I will do what you want. Please do not come here ever again.'

The visitor left silently, her head bent in shame and sorrow.

~

Arundhati was agitated. She was breathing heavily.

'Arundhati?'

No reply. She was staring into the distance, lost in thought.

'Sit down here for a minute, Arundhati,' Anupurba said apprehensively.

Still no answer.

'Arundhati . . .'

Arundhati suddenly clutched Anupurba's hand helplessly.

'Why do such things happen to me, Madam? Why is there no solution to anything in this world?'

Anupurba didn't know what to say. The curiosity of the two ayahs had spread to a few other staff members who had come out of the office to see what was going on.

Anupurba took charge now. 'Come with me, Arundhati. Sit down for a while, and then you can go. Radhika, if you see Abhay, ask him to wait here. Arundhati will return in ten minutes.'

She took Arundhati to the Art Room and made her sit down.

'Now tell me what has happened,' she said.

'That was Rosa Aunty. Samuel's wife.'

'I guessed as much. What has happened now?'

'She was here for her own need. Samuel has booked a flat. When I heard of this, I told him to transfer the ownership to me. After that, we would have nothing more to do with each other. Did I say anything that was wrong? That flat would be my only support. If I have a roof over my head, I can earn my living—I can wash utensils, if need be. I will take care of my son. But Samuel didn't agree. He shouted at me, he became violent.'

'He beat you?'

'Yes, his hands go up now at the slightest excuse. I usually suffer everything, but that day I lost my head. After he had left I went and told my neighbour what had happened. Her son is the most notorious goonda in the locality. He summoned some members of his gang and when they heard what had happened they were so enraged, they set out to kill Samuel.'

'And then?'

'I managed to stop them. I swear, Madam, it was only the thought of his wife and children that made me hold them back. I may hate Samuel but how could I have let them kill him? So I told those people—"Do what you like with him—but no violence!" I hear they have created a ring of terror around him; they have put him under mental pressure. They turn up at his office unexpectedly, threaten him publicly, visit his home at odd hours and humiliate him in the presence of his wife and children. "You have insulted our sister; we will make your life miserable!" they tell him. "Transfer your flat to her and get out of her life for ever. We can look after her."'

Anupurba was stunned.

After a brief silence Arundhati went on, 'Four or five days ago, Rosa Aunty rang me up at the school. It has been so long since I had heard her voice! How much I have cursed her all these years! Yet, I spoke to her. She didn't lose her temper at all but begged me to stop the goondas from coming to her house. Laura was grown-up now. Apparently the rogues had passed lewd comments at her and threatened to kidnap her on her way to college. The girl was terrified and had stopped going to college. But tell me, Madam; is there anything I can do? Do I have any control over these goondas? I told Rosa Aunty, "Transfer the apartment to me and I shall get out of your lives for ever." But she says there is no apartment—it is all a lie.'

'Is that correct?'

'Who knows? Maybe it is true—just a trick on Samuel's part to annoy me. Or it could be that he hasn't told Rosa Aunty about the apartment. If I had known from the start how crooked the man was, I wouldn't have had to see this miserable day.'

'If the story of the apartment is untrue, why did she call you up? Why did she come here today?'

'She keeps on saying just one thing—no harm should come to her children. I know she has no feelings for Samuel now. It isn't possible for her to have any. Still, she's a mother. I can understand her worries.'

What a complex situation! Anupurba did not know what to say to Arundhati.

But she didn't have to say anything. Arundhati composed herself and said in a confident tone, 'I have thought deeply about this whole thing. Now I have to take a final decision.'

'A final decision?'

'Enough is enough. I shall have to banish Samuel from my life. I needn't beg him for favours any longer. His family's welfare is no concern of mine. I shall bring up my Abhay. I shall do all I can for him. How long can I humiliate myself in my own eyes? God is there to look after us.'

Anupurba was amazed. Where was the source of this sudden transformation? What had produced this iron will? This self-confidence?

Arundhati got up.

'I've got to go now, Madam,' she said. 'Abhay must be waiting outside.'

'Arundhati, just one request.'

'Tell me, Madam.'

'Don't call me "Madam". Call me by my name.'

'By your name, Madam?' It was difficult to read the expression on her face.

'I would like that. "Madam" creates a vast distance between us.'

'I shall try, Madam . . . Anupurba.'

Painting by Jeevitha © Spastics Society of Karnataka

fifteen

The exhibition was almost upon them. Anupurba's stress levels were rising. There were only a few children in Anupurba's class but sometimes it became difficult for her to manage them. This was the time to choose the mats for the paintings, decide on the framing, the sequence of the exhibits—there was way too much to do in the last leg. She needed to get some additional help; she needed to meet Mrs Mathur. There was no other way out.

Mrs Mathur heard what she had to say but showed no surprise. She had a smile on her face; this was a problem she welcomed.

'I was talking to Ranjana only a few days ago about this, Anupurba.'

'About this?' Anupurba asked in surprise.

'The way you've been managing the class all by yourself is really admirable. But I think we need to give you an extra pair of hands. Another thing, the final exams are also very near. That tension will be reflected in different ways. It is something very natural. Sometimes that builds up pressure in the children. But anyway, you do need some help.'

Anupurba felt relieved. She waited to see where Mrs Mathur was going with this.

'There is one problem though, Anupurba. This is exam time and all the teachers are busy with their own classes. Even the volunteers who help the teachers have no time to breathe now. The only ones who have no exam to worry about are the folks in Room 7. What if we moved someone from there to help you?'

'That would be nice.'

'Can I give this responsibility to Arundhati?'

'Sure, you can.' Thank God, Anupurba had not complained to her about the initial setback with Arundhati!

'No, what I mean is,' Mrs Mathur hesitated for a brief second, 'other teachers have complained about Arundhati from time to time. If you have an objection, do let me know. I will try to make some other arrangement.'

'I will be quite happy if Arundhati can help me, Mrs Mathur. She has a natural affection for these children. She is very compassionate, and her personal relationship with me is excellent.'

Mrs Mathur looked at her, baffled. 'I am glad you think so!'

~

Arundhati started coming to the art class. Ever since the last conversation, she had made no mention of what was going on in her own sordid life. She seemed excited and happy and you could tell that she saw the new assignment as something positive. Anupurba did not have to give her any instructions. She just came and took over, leaving her to focus on the bigger task at hand. She was such a boon to Anupurba. Sometimes Anupurba watched her in wonder. The woman had no aversion, absolutely no hesitation in working with the children at all. Sometimes she would wipe the snot streaming from a child's nose with a piece of tissue; sometimes she wiped someone's drool. When they ran around and created trouble, she would simply chide, 'You are worse than Abhay! How much he troubles me. I hope you are not doing this on purpose. Wait till I give you all a good thrashing! I am not like your Anupurba Aunty; I will really beat you all. Now sit in one place you little devils . . .'

She and Anupurba made a great team. Everything was just perfect except that she would not call Anupurba by her name. It remained 'Anupurba Madam'. Well, still an improvement. Perhaps, later, the 'Madam' would fall away by itself. All in all, the art class got a real boost now, with Arundhati to mind the children. Then one day, while there was a class in progress as usual, a boy—maybe eight or nine—suddenly walked into the class. He did not seek anyone's permission before entering—he just walked in, went across to a table and sat down with the other children. Then he pulled a sheet of paper out of the packet lying on the table and settled down to draw. Just as if no one existed besides himself.

Anupurba was quite taken aback. She had seen the boy several times in the school—that is to say, within the school compound, in the little patch of ground that had been fenced in to form a kind of children's playground. On one side of it were the swing, the slide and the see-saw for the smaller children. That was where one could always find the boy—on the swing. His eyes wore a vacant look. They were focused on some invisible point in the distance. He was a permanent fixture there except when it rained.

He did not show signs of physical abnormality. Bright, healthy face; body and limbs that looked perfectly normal. What was he doing in Asha Jyoti? Anupurba had asked herself that question whenever she walked past the playground. Maybe he was just a drifter from the neighbourhood, who knew? But now that the boy had entered her class, she felt she needed to know and then she remembered seeing the distant figure of a woman beside him sometimes. She could be his mother. Sometimes she seemed to be speaking to him but his gaze was always away, far away. But why had this child come to her class now?

She walked up to him and said, 'Hello!'

No answer.

'What's your name?'

Silence again.

'I think you have come here by mistake. Which class are you in?'

The child went on scrawling across the sheet of paper with a pencil stub. It was neither drawing nor writing. There was no expression on his face. He didn't seem to have heard what she was saying.

'Anupurba Madam!' Arundhati called out, busy tying a scarf around Shweta's head.

'Yes, Arundhati?'

Arundhati lowered her voice. 'Say nothing to the child. Let him do what he is doing.'

'Who is he?'

'Ronnie. I'll tell you about him later.' Arundhati walked over to the other side of the room to pick up the brush that had dropped from Uma's hand.

Half an hour later, Ronnie walked out of the classroom, just as abruptly as he had walked in.

Now Arundhati walked up to Anupurba. 'Ronnie is our student,' she said.

'But he doesn't seem to have cerebral palsy,' Anupurba said.

'No. He is autistic.'

The word was new to Anupurba. 'What does "autistic" mean?' she asked.

'It means he does not know how to deal with people, they almost do not exist for him—it means he has no friends. Such children like to be left alone.'

'But aren't many kids like that?'

'No. There is a difference between being alone and being completely immersed within oneself, the way Ronnie is.'

'What's the difference?'

Arundhati thought of a reply. But there was nothing more she knew. 'I'm not sure,' she said. 'I told you what I had heard.'

'Very well, I'll ask Ranjana or Shobha to explain.'

'You can ask Bani Madam too,' Arundhati said. 'Ronnie is one her pupils. He's in the sixth standard.'

'But he never attends class. How does he get promoted from one class to the next?'

'I don't quite know, Anupurba Madam.'

~

Bani gave Anupurba all the answers she wanted.

'You want to know how autistic children are different from children who like to be left alone? If an ordinary child wants to be left alone, it's only a passing feeling. Or, sometimes it may be because the child has had some experience which makes her want to build a wall around herself. But an autistic child cannot set up normal relationships with others even if she wants to. Not even with her parents or siblings.'

'Why does this happen?'

'No one knows. It's not as though this question hasn't been researched. A lot of research is still going on. From what is known, infection could be a major cause. If the mother picks up a viral infection during her pregnancy, this can sometimes lead to autism for the baby.'

'Is it curable?'

'It may or may not be. Some people believe therapy or special schools can help autistic children to pick up social skills. It has been found that in some cases they don't need to continue going to special schools.'

'So Ronnie could become normal some day?'

'That's what is being attempted here. That is the hope.'

'How is his promotion to the next class decided? Does he learn anything in school? I see him on the swing always.'

Bani laughed. 'You will never guess how intelligent he is! He may not come to class regularly, but when he wants to, he can go through his textbooks effortlessly and answer all questions. He is a genius.'

'Really?'

'Not just that. Ronnie writes beautiful poetry.'

'Poetry? Ronnie?'

'Yes. In fact, Mrs Mathur is trying to get them published as an anthology some day.'

Anupurba said a small prayer to herself as she left Bani. 'Heal the child, dear God! Whoever you are, wherever you may be—make him all right. Do not keep him alone like this. Don't you feel what he feels, God? Don't you see him on the swing?'

She felt desperate to do something, anything for Ronnie. But in the next moment, she felt helpless. She walked away slowly, wanting only to be left alone with her thoughts.

~

The very next day that she came to Asha Jyoti, Anupurba's eyes strayed to the playground. As on most other days, Ronnie was there on the swing. The lady she had seen before stood near him.

On a sudden impulse, Anupurba walked up to them.

'Hello!' she said.

'Hello!'

'I'm Anupurba, I volunteer here. And you are Ronnie's . . .'

'Mother.'

'I've seen you here often. Do you spend the whole day with him in the school?'

'Yes, there is no other way. If Ronnie could sit still in class, it would have been different. But he is quite likely to walk out of the class whenever he feels like—it is an impulse. When he gets on the swing he simply refuses to get off. One has to keep an eye on him. He has involuntary movements sometimes; he can get hurt very badly.'

'Ronnie walked into my class quite unexpectedly the other day.'

'Which class do you teach?'

'The art class.'

'Ronnie can't draw at all,' his mother said, laughing. 'But he writes beautiful poetry. Would you like to have a look?'

She pulled a diary out of her purse. It contained a few poems. The lines were crooked, the letters uneven in size; capital letters mingled with small case letters. She read the first poem:

Morpheus, can you tell me
How to grapple with the pain of growing up
With the anguish of knowing that razor passion is lost
And the mind is numbed.
To know that you will not jump off the cliff ever again,
Kiss your borders with holy lips,

Embrace your friend so hard that it hurts.
Not to feel the burning glory of youth,
The ever tapping feet,
The thrust to squeeze life, drop by drop
The crusade of stealing fire to turn it into
fiery blossoms!

Anupurba was stunned. How could this small boy write such beautiful lines?

'I haven't given up hope. People say writing can help autistic children to connect with others. Through it, they are more likely to become normal some day. Let us see what the future holds for us!'

It was time for her class to begin. Anupurba walked towards the Art Room. But she was unable to forget the lines held together in Ronnie's crooked handwriting. *Stealing fire*, she repeated in her head, *to turn it into fiery blossoms. . . .*

~

The next day, as Anupurba was walking towards her classroom, Ronnie's mother rushed up to her like a storm, with a pile of newspapers in her hand.

'Excuse me, Anupurba!' She was out of breath.

'Hello! How come you are here?' Anupurba's looked around, Ronnie was not in sight.

'I had to show you something,' Ronnie's mother said, waving a newspaper at her.

'What is in it?'

Her eyes shone. 'Open it and see,' she said.

Curious, Anupurba spread out the pages. It was *The Hindu*.

Ronnie's mother could not wait. 'Turn to the Art and Literature Supplement,' she said.

She turned the pages.

Then she saw it—across the top of the page was a large photograph of Ronnie and several of his poems had been published below it.

'I had never dreamt that Ronnie's poems would be published some day,' his mother said. 'It's all due to Mrs Mathur. Some journalists had come to interview her. Later, she took them round the school and the Health Centre and also told them about Ronnie. She sent for me and asked me to show them Ronnie's diary. After that, two of them descended on our house, asking to see all his writings. And now this! I bought out all the copies the newspaper hawker had. I want you to have this one. You needn't return it. So long!'

She ran back. She seemed to have grown wings.

Mother of a son who had not called her 'Mother' even once.

Anupurba sighed. Then she entered the classroom.

Painting by Vivethitha © Spastics Society of Karnataka

sixteen

Lunch break wasn't over yet. The children had not returned but Arundhati had already arranged everything. Anupurba experienced a surge of affection for this woman who would have to spend her entire life atoning for that one single lapse.

Life was bound to have become difficult for her after banishing Samuel—at least financially. But she did not see any trace of the struggle on her face, the bitterness that had become her constant companion was completely gone in a few weeks. Her future was as uncertain as ever; she didn't know how she was going to survive if her temporary job was to go away. But peace seemed to have returned to her.

'Ah, here's Anupurba Madam! I have arranged all the paintings on this table. Today we should decide the sequence in which you want them displayed at the exhibition.'

Anupurba took another look at the children's paintings. She rearranged some. As she was rearranging the sequence one more time, she said, 'We should show them once to Mrs Mathur and Ranjana.'

'Shall I ask them to come and have a look after school is over today?'

'Yes, go tell them.'

Arundhati left.

The children began to arrive. Their excitement knew no bounds. They had a thousand questions for her, especially about the exhibition. Who all were expected to come? Would anyone actually buy their paintings? What would happen if they remained unsold? Would there be no more art classes next year? If they continued, would Anupurba Aunty stay on? Or would they have a new Aunty? Anupurba could never have managed them without Arundhati's help.

'Yes, they say they will come!' said Arundhati, coming back into the class.

Arundhati returned to what she was doing—adjusting someone's wheelchair, stroking someone else to calm her down, putting a paint-brush in another child's hand. You needed to have ten hands to function in this place!

'Oh no!' Lata shouted out suddenly.

Both Anupurba and Arundhati rushed to her side. 'What's the matter, Lata?'

'I can't get it right! It's not happening!' She was screaming now.

Not just today, but from the very day that the art classes had begun, Anupurba had noticed that Lata wasn't ever satisfied with her own drawing. Perhaps her crippled and helpless fingers were unable to capture the images that crowded her mind. Anupurba had spent a great deal of time trying to explain things to her. 'It's okay,' she would say. But Lata silently dismissed her. She knew nothing was okay.

'Who said it is not happening?' Anupurba said enthusiastically. 'Your work is so wonderful!'

'No, it isn't! No one will even look at my painting!'

Anupurba's enthusiasm failed to convince Lata.

All of a sudden, Anupurba felt apprehensive. Were the children becoming too tense? Had she over-pitched the whole exhibition thing? With the event next week, who knew how pressured they felt inside?

Arundhati put down a bottle of green paint, which she had made by mixing blue and yellow colours, in front of Lata.

'Now colour those plants green!' she said.

'No, I won't!' Lata shouted. 'It's no use! Take it a-w-a-y-.' She picked up the bottle of paint in her crippled hands and threw it to her right, where Arundhati had arranged all the paintings on a small table. Then she pushed her chair aside and walked out of the classroom sobbing loudly and uncontrollably.

The other children in the class seemed to have turned into statues. So did Anupurba and Arundhati.

But it was Arundhati who recovered first. She ran to the table with a box of tissues and dabbed away at the green paint splattered across the children's paintings.

Anupurba was silent. In a helpless stupor she watched months of hard work destroyed in a single moment!

Neither Anupurba nor Arundhati knew when the bell rang and the class ended. Luckily, Lata's deformed hand lacked strength and so the paintings on the far side had not been affected. But the paintings on one side were ruined.

Anupurba held up a painting in her hand. It was one of Raja's. Although Anupurba had not spoken to anyone about it, she knew this was the pick of all the paintings. It was also the one that had suffered the most damage. There were large green splashes on the delicate watercolours. There was no way one could repair them.

'What happened?' Mrs Mathur asked as she entered the classroom with Ranjana.

Anupurba did not reply but moved slightly to one side. She still could not speak. There was something stuck in her throat. She covered her lips tightly with the fingers of her right hand; she did not trust herself.

'Who did this?' Ranjana asked. She realized that the pictures had been vandalized.

Arundhati said haltingly, 'Lata got angry and flung a bottle of paint.'

'Lata!' Both Mrs Mathur and Ranjana were surprised.

Whatever else she was, Lata wasn't known to be given to fits of ill temper. What could have made her do such a thing?

There was no time to discuss what had happened or even to worry about it. They all got busy trying to remove the splashes of green paint on pictures that still had some hope. It took them a long time.

Anupurba rearranged the paintings on the table.

'What shall we do now? The exhibition can't begin on schedule.' She was speaking to no one in particular.

'Why not?' It was Mrs Mathur.

'How can we show these splattered paintings? Just a handful has been saved . . .'

'Anupurba, this is Asha Jyoti's exhibition, not an exhibition by a famous art gallery,' Ranjana said. 'No one will come here to see a Husain or a Gujral. Those who come will know the background; they will come because they have sympathy for us. For such people, even the flaws will be strengths. We will go ahead; we will have our exhibition on schedule. Believe me, we have enough in here. Don't worry at all.'

'Yes,' said Mrs Mathur dramatically. 'Let's roll.'

Painting by Farooq © Spastics Society of Karnataka

seventeen

Shobha was so busy—almost as though she was a wedding coordinator or something. She was running around, printing the invitations, mailing them, going to several places to deliver them in person, speaking to press people, informing all the parents, getting the event schedule rehearsed. She was everywhere. Over the weekend, Anupurba finally caught up with her on the phone to see how things were.

'You will be thrilled with the turnout,' Shobha said.

Anupurba did not want to think about it. She was not swayed easily and would believe it when she saw it. After the Lata fiasco, she simply kept her fingers crossed.

'Shobha, did you invite Shubhendu?' she asked.

'No, they will not come.'

'Why not? Wouldn't this be a good way to soften Reena?'

'No, Purba. They are leaving town. Forever,' Shobha replied. There was no emotion in her voice. 'They will be gone soon. They decided to pack up and leave.'

Anupurba did not say anything.

~

While they were all waiting outside to receive the Chief Guest on the first day of the exhibition, Ranjana came and quietly stood beside Anupurba.

'There is something I want to tell you,' she whispered.

'Tell me,' Anupurba said.

'Prashant has got a transfer to Bangalore.'

'Who? Oh, my God! Prashant!' Anupurba realized in an instant who she was referring to.

'Aren't you going to congratulate me?' Ranjana was in bliss.

'Oh Ranjana, I can't tell you how happy I am. Congratulations.' She hugged her and as she suddenly remembered something, she said, 'So, now you won't have to leave Asha Jyoti. It's wonderful. This school needs you so much.'

Ranjana smiled. 'No, the question of my leaving Asha Jyoti doesn't arise any more. It's such a load off my mind! I was only trying to be brave when I told you that I would go away after my marriage, but I wasn't at peace with myself . . . But you'll be gone soon, won't you? It was so nice to have you here . . .'

Anupurba felt sad. The friendship between them would have taken years to blossom in some other setting. Now she would have to leave all this behind!

'How wonderful it would be if you . . .' Ranjana started

to say something but the sentence remained unfinished. The Chief Guest's car had arrived.

The Chief Guest was Bangalore's celebrated artist, Madhuri Basappa. Her paintings were routinely exhibited in Paris and Manhattan. That year she had received the Padma Bhushan. The camera crew surged forward.

Mrs Mathur escorted her into the exhibition hall. Anupurba deliberately kept herself in the background. How would Madhuri Basappa react to the paintings, she wondered. She might applaud, just to please her hosts—or she might not deign to do even that. A plain-speaking artist, she might say bluntly, 'These children have to work much harder. The paintings are not bad, but they could be far better.' If she said such a thing, the children would feel so discouraged.

'Excuse me!'

Anupurba turned around. The man talking to her was fair-complexioned and tall. His hair was prematurely grey, but he did not look a day over forty. There was a cultured air about him. Where had she seen the gentleman before? At Asha Jyoti? Or was it at some party? The face looked so familiar.

'Yes?'

'Are you a teacher here?' he asked, glancing at the badge round her neck.

'No, just a volunteer,' she replied.

'I had a few questions to ask about this exhibition,' the man said. 'I don't know who to ask. Could you . . .'

'You can ask me,' she said. 'I might be able to answer

your questions. Why don't I show you the paintings?'

He pulled a pencil and a sheet of paper out of his pocket as he followed her. Was he a journalist? But the press conference had taken place a day earlier. Most newspapers had carried the reports.

The gentleman studied each painting in the exhibition carefully, from the first to the last, asking very specific questions. Who was the artist? How old was he or she? What disability did the artist have?

'May I ask you one question? What organization do you represent?' Anupurba finally asked, unable to restrain her curiosity.

'Oh, I am from a software company . . .'

Someone from a software company taking so much interest in paintings by the children of Asha Jyoti?

He folded the sheet of paper and put it back in his pocket. Then, in an admiring tone, he said, 'I see you are very knowledgeable about these paintings.'

Anupurba did not want to explain her role in the exhibition; she only said, 'Thank you!'

'One last question. How does one buy these paintings?'

'You would have to see our Public Relations Officer, Shobha, for that. Would you like to speak to her now? I can call her.'

'Please.'

'Shobha, can you come here for a minute?' Anupurba called out and as soon as Shobha saw the man with her, she came with long strides from across the hall.

'Mr Rathore! What a pleasant surprise! I never thought you would find the time to come here! Thank you so much for coming! Let me introduce you to our Principal.'

Shobha led Mr Rathore away to the spot where Mrs Mathur was talking to Madhuri Basappa. After a few moments, she returned quickly to Anupurba.

'Purba, what was Mr Rathore asking you?' She was as excited as a schoolgirl.

'Who is this Mr Rathore?' Anupurba asked.

'You haven't heard of Ranbir Rathore?'

'Which Ranbir Rathore?' Anupurba asked. Then she remembered. 'You mean the person who has set up that huge software company in Bangalore? He's in the papers almost every day!' No wonder the face looked familiar.

'How come he was here? Did you invite him?'

'Yes, I did. I've been going around handing out invitations to all and sundry. Who knows—someone may turn out to be a Good Samaritan. But you tell me now—what was he asking you?'

'He went around the exhibition and looked at everything closely. Asked me dozens of questions about the children whose paintings are exhibited here. Finally, he asked how he could buy some of these paintings. That was why I called you.'

Shobha's face lit up.

'It would be wonderful for us if Ranbir Rathore bought some of the paintings. It would give us a lot of publicity and that would attract other buyers.'

Madhuri Basappa spent some time at the exhibition and then left. But Ranbir Rathore stayed on, chatting away with the children, occasionally holding a child's hand or stroking a child's head. He was in no hurry.

Finally, just as he was leaving, he said something to Mrs Mathur and Ranjana in a low voice and got into his car. Anupurba was observing them from a distance. She could not catch the words, but she did see Mrs Mathur look astounded. What could he have said, she wondered.

As soon as the car drove away, an excited Mrs Mathur waved to Shobha and Anupurba. She obviously wanted to tell them something of great importance.

'What happened, Mrs Mathur?' Anupurba asked eagerly.

'Thank you, Anupurba! You are an angel!'

Anupurba could only stare at her.

'Ranbir Rathore says he will buy up all the paintings that have remained unsold at the exhibition. But not at the price we want. "You ladies are not cut out for business," he told me, "these paintings are priceless."'

'Anupurba, he was completely charmed by the way you described the paintings to him and explained the feelings of each child behind every painting,' said Ranjana and hugged her.

'I haven't given you the all-important news yet, Anupurba.' It was Mrs Mathur. 'Mr Rathore's company will sponsor the school's art department!'

'What do you mean art department?'

'They will get a new building constructed. Only for art! And they will pay the salaries! They will provide everything we need—furniture, art materials, everything!'

So much! Now it was Anupurba's turn to be overwhelmed.

'That's not all, Anupurba! His company will buy up everything that our children paint! Their paintings will be hung in all the company's offices, in every part of the world! He has asked me to send Shobha to his office soon; he wants everything finalized on paper, copyright ownership and all that stuff.'

~

It was the last day of the exhibition. Anupurba would soon be free now. No need to rush to Asha Jyoti on Mondays and Thursdays. Her work was over.

She should be glad. But somehow, she was feeling weighed down. As though she was going to part with something precious. She searched her mind for the reason.

Mrs Mathur came and flopped down in a chair next to hers after she had escorted an important guest to his car.

'Thank you so much, Anupurba!' she said. 'The exhibition wouldn't have gone off so well but for you.'

'What are you saying, Mrs Mathur?' Anupurba said, embarrassed. 'What did I do? It was the children who did everything! And it was you, Ranjana and Shobha who made all the arrangements.'

'That isn't true, Anupurba,' Mrs Mathur said. She was silent for a moment; she was thinking what words to use. Then she said haltingly, 'There is something I wanted to ask of you.'

'Please ask, Mrs Mathur.'

'You've heard about Mr Rathore's offer. This summer we can get the Art Wing ready. When the school reopens in June, we can hold proper art classes in a spacious hall, not in that tiny room. Can't you take charge of the new wing, Anupurba?'

'Me?'

Thinking that the expression on her face indicated hesitation, Mrs Mathur said, 'And not as a volunteer. I would like you to join the school as a regular teacher.'

'Mrs Mathur, how can I carry such a big responsibility all by myself?'

Mrs Mathur thought for a moment. 'You're quite right,' she said. 'We'll have to find someone who can help you. Full time. The art department won't be short of funds now. After you've agreed, I'll have to advertise. Then you can select someone yourself.'

'There's no need to advertise, Mrs Mathur.'

'No?'

'No.'

Mrs Mathur waited to hear what she would say.

'I'm ready to join Asha Jyoti whenever you want, Mrs Mathur. And as for the assistant, I already have one. She merely has to be given a permanent appointment.'

'Who are you talking about?' Mrs Mathur could probably already guess, though.

'Why, Arundhati, of course! Can I find anyone better?'

The two looked at each other without a word. It was Shobha who broke the silence. 'This calls for a celebration, Mrs Mathur.'

'Of course. My place, tonight,' Shanta Mathur replied with the enthusiasm of someone half her age.

'No, Mrs Mathur, my place!' It was Anupurba. She smiled. 'This time it is my turn.'

Author's Note

It was a December day, just before Christmas. At the school for children with cerebral palsy run by the Spastics Society of Karnataka, there was a Christmas party for the students. With some hesitation and considerable misgiving, I had come with my husband, Subroto. It was here at this party that I first observed, at close quarters, children crippled by cerebral palsy.

After an hour of merry-making, the party ended with a dance. The children danced to the tune of a popular Hindi film song, although the rhythm was somewhat ragged; and with them danced the staff and some of the parents and the invited guests. I was unable to join in. My legs had turned to stone. Just then, a little girl tugged at my hand, 'Come, Aunty, let's dance!'

I cannot describe what happened to me as I swung across the floor holding on to that little crippled hand. I started sobbing uncontrollably, tears streamed from my eyes, unchecked.

Just the way it happens to Anupurba.

I returned to the school a few days later to buy handmade greeting cards which the children had created. There I met the Principal, Mrs Rukmini Krishnaswami. As we were talking, she said, 'I am told that you are a writer. Why don't you write about our children? No one understands them or really knows anything about them. Some, out of ignorance, even call them mad. I want them to know that most of our children are perfectly normal mentally, though they may be physically disabled.'

'But I write only in Oriya,' I replied. 'It's a regional language with very limited readership. Things may not turn out as you expect.'

'So?' she countered. 'At least some people will get to know. Later, someone may even translate the work into another language. And who knows, perhaps an English translation . . .'

I was surprised at her optimism.

For some time, I thought over what she had said. Then one day, I decided to write a novel on the children with cerebral palsy, their families and their care-givers. I told myself that I would fictionalize the characters and some events but be faithful to the issues, the struggle, the disappointments and the dreams of the children and those who took care of them. There would be nothing fictional about that.

I spent the next few months mostly at the Spastics Society of Karnataka. My companion during those days was Latika, who was a teacher at the school. With her help, I got to know many teachers, parents, doctors, counsellors and voluntary workers. The experience touched me deeply.

That was about seven years ago.

One thing followed another, but I could not get on with the writing of the novel. My experiences at the school lay buried deep in my mind, perhaps waiting for the right moment to be strung together in a single narrative.

Then suddenly it happened. As I sat down to write, it was as if it wasn't I but someone else that was writing; I was being driven by some powerful emotion.

A few days after the novel was completed, Subroto and I were invited to the wedding of Latika's eldest son. There I ran into Mrs Krishnaswami. She had aged some, she looked a little older and now held a stick for support, but her eyes had the same glow that I had seen seven years back.

'Have you written the book yet?' she asked me.

I was amazed that after all these years she still remembered.

'I have just finished writing it,' I replied. 'And God willing, it will soon be published.'

Her face shone. 'I'm sure He has willed it,' she said. 'Do you know something?' she added. 'The Spastics Society of Karnataka will celebrate its Silver Jubilee this year! I have a feeling your book is timed for that.'

I could say nothing at the time. But today Mrs Rukmini Krishnaswami's words are about to come true. *Deba Shishu* is getting ready, in time for the Silver Jubilee year of the Spastics Society of Karnataka. How I wish my pen could capture even a fragment of the joy that my heart feels!

Susmita Bagchi
December 2006